TWIST MY CHARM

Love Potion #11

Books by Toni Gallagher

TWIST MY CHARM

The Popularity Spell
Love Potion #11

TWIST MY CHARM

Love Potion #11

TONI GALLAGHER

Random House 🏠 New York

Text copyright © 2016 by Toni Gallagher
Jacket art copyright © 2016 by Helen Huang

All rights reserved. Published in the United States by
Random House Children's Books, a division of Penguin Random House LLC, New York.

Random House and the colophon are registered trademarks of Penguin Random House LLC.

Visit us on the Web! randomhousekids.com

Educators and librarians, for a variety of teaching tools,
visit us at RHTeachersLibrarians.com

Library of Congress Cataloging-in-Publication Data
Names: Gallagher, Toni.
Title: Love potion #11 / Toni Gallagher.
Other titles: Love potion number eleven
Description: First edition. | New York : Random House, [2016] Series: Twist my charm ; [2]
Summary: "Cleo and her friends get into matchmaking mischief when she receives
a love potion recipe" —Provided by publisher.
Identifiers: LCCN 2015019925 | ISBN 978-0-553-51119-2 (trade) |
ISBN 978-0-553-51120-8 (lib. bdg.) | ISBN 978-0-553-51121-5 (ebook)
Subjects: | CYAC: Love—Fiction. | Magic—Fiction. | Interpersonal relations—Fiction. |
Middle schools—Fiction. | Schools—Fiction. | Humorous stories. | BISAC: JUVENILE
FICTION / Girls & Women. | JUVENILE FICTION / Social Issues / Friendship. |
JUVENILE FICTION / Humorous Stories.
Classification: LCC PZ7.G355 Lo 2016 | DDC [Fic]—dc23

Printed in the United States of America
10 9 8 7 6 5 4 3 2 1
First Edition

To Max.
Wishing you all the friendship and love that
this magical world has to offer!

TWIST MY CHARM

Love Potion #11

1

"It's disgusting."

"It's offensive."

"It should not be allowed on school grounds!"

"Our brains are still forming; we should not be in the presence of this kind of activity!"

"There should be a rule against it."

"There should be a *law* against it!"

Madison Paddington and I are in perfect agreement. There's nothing ickier than two sixth graders acting like they're in love.

Across the lunchroom, Madison's former-but-still-kinda friend Lisa Lee is tossing her hair back, giggling like a girly hyena at something Ronnie Cheseboro just said. Nothing can be *that* funny. Especially from Ronnie. He thinks burping is hilarious and hocking loogies is even better.

"Are they calling themselves boyfriend and girlfriend?"

I ask Madison as I cut my meatloaf and pop a piece into my mouth.

"No, Lisa Lee says they're *hanging out.*"

I chew and think about this. Now, I hang out all the time. Well, not *all* the time, but on the weekends, and after school when Dad lets me. Still, since I moved to Los Angeles from Ohio almost a year ago, most of my hanging out has been with Madison. And before her, I hung out with my used-to-be-but-not-really-anymore friend Samantha.

That's *friendly* hanging out, though. That's not what Madison is talking about. She means boys.

I don't want to hang out like *that* anytime soon, especially if you have to laugh at burps and loogies or care about sports and video games. Yawn!

Madison says that once you turn twelve you start thinking more about hanging out with boys, but she celebrated the big one-two before we were friends and she doesn't care about boys yet . . . I don't think.

"You don't care about boys now, do you?" I ask.

"Ewww, no. At least not anybody at school. Why? Do *you* like somebody?"

"No way!" I say. "I'm still eleven."

"Yeah, but you're the only one here who has a love potion!"

"Shhh!" I hiss at her. "The LP is not to be discussed on school grounds."

For someone who doesn't care about boys, Madison is

very interested in my love potion. I can't blame her. It's a cool thing to have, for sure. My uncle Arnie sent it to me as a gift when I performed in *Healthyland,* a play at school. Most kids get flowers or cards or gift cards to iTunes, but that's not his way. He lives in New Orleans and has a head of big, frizzy hair like Albert Einstein and a cat called Fuzzer who looks exactly like him. The best explanation of Uncle Arnie is that he's the kind of person who thinks a voodoo doll is a good birthday gift for an eleven-year-old.

It wasn't.

Madison never totally believed that the voodoo doll worked, but she's always bringing up my love potion. It's part of the reason I think she must like a boy—maybe not here at Friendship Community School, but somewhere.

She lowers her voice and leans in. "Has your uncle told you how it works yet?"

I dunk some mashed potatoes into the lake of gravy in the middle. "Not yet."

Uncle Arnie's note said "instructions to follow," and I've been waiting for them ever since. It's hard for me to wait for things; I like things to happen right now. But I'm in a class at school called Focus! that teaches us how to deal with things like being patient, and I guess it's working, because I haven't called or texted or emailed Uncle Arnie once to ask him about the love potion. More than twenty-one whole days, and I haven't done a thing . . . except think and think and think about it, day and night, awake and in dreams, on school days and weekends, all the time! To tell the truth, I'm about to burst.

"Darn," Madison says. "It'd be fun to try on someone here at school."

Someone at school? That *would* be fun! "Who?" I ask.

"I don't know." She looks around the lunchroom, and her eyes stop at her old table in front of the big window, the one she used to share with Lisa Lee and Kylie Mae. Kylie Mae is sitting down now too, giggling with Lonnie Cheseboro, Ronnie's twin brother. Ickiness doubled! "Maybe Ronnie . . . or Lonnie."

"They don't need a love potion. They've got Lisa Lee and Kylie Mae. They're already *in loooove*." I make my voice nice and sarcastic so Madison knows how I feel about it.

"Yeah, but wouldn't it be fun if one of them fell in love with Janet?"

Ha! Janet teaches our phys ed class, but our school calls it Recreational Wellness, because they're weird that way. I like the idea of Ronnie or Lonnie falling in love with Janet, but I have a better one. "How about the class ferret?"

We watch as Ronnie wads up his brown paper lunch bag and tosses it, basketball-style, into a huge trash can a few feet away from him. The girls cheer as he and his brother high-five each other with loud smacks like they just won at the X Games.

"He could fall in love with that trash can," I suggest.

Madison laughs. "A boy and his trash can. A love story for all time."

As we're laughing, our friend Larry plops himself into the chair next to mine, his lunch tray clattering onto the table. Like he does every day, he opens the outside pocket of his backpack and pulls out Mono (*"Rhymes with oh no,"* he always says), a little wooden monkey sculpture about four inches high. It's ridiculously adorable, with carved black-painted "fur" surrounding a mischievous face of "fur" painted white. He got it when his parents took him on a jungle adventure tour in Costa Rica for spring break, and now this monkey is always by his side. It's part of what makes Larry Larry.

"So, what's the rating on the meatloaf?" he asks. "Edible, or time to call the health department?"

I give it an A-minus. He takes a bite of his and agrees.

As we're talking, Samantha crosses the lunchroom and walks past us, holding a tray with the same lunch on it. I open my mouth to say something. Any words could work. *Hey, the lunch is good today. You're gonna like those potatoes. Want to sit with us?* But nothing comes out. I've barely said anything to Sam since we fought over my voodoo doll. We talked after the play—I even gave her a hug—but the most conversation we've had since then is when we happen to be near each other and say, "Hey."

I want to be friends with Sam again, but I don't even

know where to start. How can you be friends with some-one when she's announced you're no longer friends . . . and thrown pepperoni on you in the lunchroom . . . and chased you through a graveyard?

I don't have the answer to that, so all I do lately is say, "Hey." And today I didn't even do that.

"So, what's the hot topic at the lunch table today, ladies?" Larry asks. He never says something normal, like "What's up?"

Madison and I look at each other. We agreed to keep the love potion between us, so we scramble for a safer answer.

"Lisa Lee and Kylie Mae," I say.

"And Ronnie and Lonnie Cheseboro," Madison adds. "They're hanging out, you know, like couples."

"Two girls talking about two other girls in love with two lame-o guys?" Larry says. "Snoresville! I expected a lot more out of you two. Art, literature, or at least the advan-tages of enjoying Friendship Community School lunch as a sandwich cookie."

Larry's holding up two pieces of meatloaf with mashed potatoes in between. He lifts it to his mouth like a ham-burger and takes a big bite. Then, with his mouth full, he adds, "Work on something better for lunch tomorrow, please."

We crack up and promise him we will.

2

After school Yvonne the "au pair" picks us up and drives us to Madison's house. Madison doesn't have a nanny anymore; she has this blond college-age girl from Finland who's more like a driver and tutor and general all-around helper. Dad said he'd like an au pair for his life too . . . until he found out they get paid.

Pulling up to Madison's house is like arriving at a castle. There's no moat or drawbridge, but there's a big gate that opens with the touch of a button, leading to a wide circular driveway. Most people—like me—would call it a mansion. Even a princess would dream of having a room like Madison's, with its pink wallpaper and canopy bed, a little table with a mirror and chair, lots of open space, and no junk on the floor. My favorite part of her room is the big white sliding door that opens to a balcony with a patio overlooking her backyard. It's as pretty as a city park out there, with shrubs and flowers and a perfectly cut lawn—not like my backyard, which is mostly dirt with patchy grass peppered with poop from my awesome Irish setter, Toby. Madison doesn't have a dog, which is too bad because her parents would probably pay someone to do nothing but be a poop picker-upper.

Standing on Madison's balcony, I raise my hand and wave slowly, making a figure eight in the air. I'm like a queen looking over my kingdom and its subjects—though my only subject right now is a guy in a baseball cap skimming Madison's sparkling blue pool. He waves back.

Oh well, having one subject is enough for now, I guess.

"Hey, I thought you were gonna help me with my art project!" Madison says, joining me on the balcony. Then she tosses something on the floor that makes a slurpy, sloshy sound.

I look down. It's a green bucket filled with lumpy white gloop. It looks like oatmeal someone ate that came up again, and I can tell just by looking at it that it's cold and clammy and sticky and gross.

"We've got to rip up newspaper into strips and dip them in that," she tells me.

I look down again. I don't mind creepy and crawly or dirty and dusty, but this gloppy, gloopy concoction immediately makes me sick to my stomach.

"You want me to put my hands in that?" I ask. "I seriously might barf."

I really might.

Madison doesn't believe me. "You? You don't even mind a slimy millipede crawling on your arm!"

That *is* true. Millie the millipede is my favorite pet. Well, my equal favorite with Toby, of course. "But Millie is cute!" I say in a voice dangerously close to a whine. "That"—I point to the glop—"is not cute."

"You said you'd help me," says Madison. "I only just came up with this idea, and I'm behind. I can't do it all alone."

"What are you making anyway?" I ask, trying to delay this a little longer. She runs back into her room and returns to the balcony with an oval made of chicken wire, about the size of a watermelon, partially covered with strips of newspaper.

"What is it?" I ask.

"It's papier-mâché."

"I know that. But *what* is it?"

"I'll tell you later, when it's further along," she promises. With that, she plops herself on the tile patio, rips a piece of newspaper, and plunges it into the bucket.

I watch her flatten the paper onto the chicken wire. "Well, I wish you'd picked something less disgusting," I say. Our school's art show—named the Immersive Interactive Art Installation (nothing is simple at Friendship Community School)—is coming up in two weeks, and the project I chose is simple and neat: storyboards. Storyboards are drawings that show a movie director how each scene is going to look—like a super-detailed graphic novel or comic book. We saw some in Madison's dad's office when we sneaked in to look at his People's Choice Award. My movie is only in my imagination so far, but it will star my favorite character that I created: Pandaroo, an intergalactic bear who propels himself through space by farting rainbows.

Madison places another piece of newspaper onto her chicken wire and pats it down neatly. She plunges both hands back into the bucket and lifts them up, white glop dripping disgustingly between her fingers. With a pretend evil laugh she asks, "So, are you going to help me . . . or do you want to be covered in this stuff?"

I slowly stand up. "What I want to do is . . . get out of here!" I run off the patio into her bedroom, hoping my sneakers won't smudge her ultra-shiny hardwood floors. I hide in the closet, which is the size of most people's bedrooms . . . or living rooms . . . or houses. Madison's T-shirts are color-coordinated, her jeans are neatly piled in individual cubbyholes, and every shoe is matched with its partner, lined up on shelves. It's a long way from my bedroom, where T-shirts are shoved unfolded into a drawer and jeans are usually wadded up on the floor next to Toby.

Even though nobody wears winter coats in Los Angeles, Madison's closet has a whole row of them. It's a great place to hide! I squeeze in between two puffy parkas. Their fur hoods tickle both sides of my face, and I try not to laugh as I wait for her to find me.

But *I* find something first.

Underneath a low-hanging rod filled with blouses are two . . . eyes.

Human eyes.

For a second I think they might belong to a real person. You never know at Madison's house, with its housekeepers and pool cleaners and handymen around all the time. But why would any of them be silently chilling on the floor of her closet?

"Hello?" I ask quietly. This can't be a person, but I'm still cautious as I take a step forward. The eyes don't move or blink or close. I take a deep breath, step closer, and push the blouses apart.

Turns out it's not one pair of eyes but a bunch of them.

Leaning against the wall is a poster board collage, filled with photos from top to bottom, from left to right. They're all pictures of the same boy in different sizes, some in black and white, but most in color. Sometimes in a baseball cap or a knit beanie, sometimes showing off a head of spiky blond hair. Smiling with glistening white teeth in some, serious in others. His eyes are blue . . . or green . . . or hazel . . . it's hard to say, but one thing is for sure—they are the most beautiful eyes I've ever seen. He is cuuuuuuute. This must be the boy Madison likes! Why would she be interested in one of the dopey doofuses at school when she's known about this boy for who knows how long?

"Cleo, where are you?" Madison's voice sounds nearby.

I pick up the collage and walk out of the closet. "Who . . . is . . . this?"

A worried look crosses Madison's face. "Oh. I didn't really want you to see that yet."

"Why not?"

"Ummm, because you'd think I was a total dork."

I stare at her and tell her the ultimate truth. "I could never think that, not in a million billion years." If Madison tried to dress for Halloween as a "total dork," it's the one outfit she could never pull off. For me, the costume would be pretty easy. I'd put on my usual clothes and smile real big.

"You don't? Think I'm a dork?" she asks.

"Of course not!"

Madison seems relieved as she lays the collage on the floor between us. I know they're only pictures, but I feel weird inside, having this boy's many faces all this close to me. For some reason it feels . . . embarrassing.

"So . . . who is he?" I ask.

Madison looks at the poster board dreamily. "Wow. I don't even know how to begin to explain Ryder Landry."

"That's this boy?"

"Oh, he's more than a boy," she says seriously. "He's a huge singer. He writes the most awesome songs, and not just pop stuff. Some of them are deep and meaningful and unbelievable." As she fills me in, she walks into her closet and comes back with a bunch more collages. "He's on TV all the time and online and in magazines. He's everywhere!"

I don't bother explaining that Dad and I don't have a movie theater screen and a billion cable channels like she does—that we only watch stuff on the Internet, usually Japanese anime or new shows from England or Finland. And Dad listens to boring podcasts and songs from the eighties, not normal radio music.

"*He's* what I'm making for the art show," Madison tells me. "Out on the patio. That's going to be his head."

"I love that idea!" I say, but the Friendship Community School Immersive Interactive Art Installation is the farthest thing from my mind as I stare at photo after photo on Madison's poster board, and Ryder's eyes melt into mine.

"Let me show you a video!" Madison runs over to her computer, and with the quick click of a button, I'm seeing Ryder Landry onstage. A song is ending, and a huge auditorium full of kids—mostly girls but boys too—is exploding with screams and cheers. I can hear Madison saying words next to me—something about going to a concert once with Lisa Lee and Kylie Mae—but I'm not really paying attention. I can't take my eyes off Ryder, who's moving like a panther or a puma, prowling gracefully through the jungle.

"Thank you, everybody," he says. His voice makes me think of a river of warm honey that, for some reason, I want to swim in. The crowd quiets down when he brings the microphone to his mouth and talks like he knows them personally. "I know what it's like for all of you out there," he says, "because I've been through it too. I've had my problems, my struggles. I've moved, I've changed schools. . . ."

Me too! I'm still kind of a new kid at Friendship Community, after all.

"I've lost people who are important to me. . . ."

Me too! My mom died when I was little, and I grew up with just my dad. Then right when I started to like his girlfriend, Terri, she broke up with him, so I sort of lost her too. I can't believe how much Ryder and I have in common.

"I've known love and I've had my heart broken. . . ."

Okay, well, he's got me there. I mean, I love my dad and Toby and Millie, and I guess my uncle Arnie, but I don't think that's what Ryder's talking about.

"This song goes out to all of you."

The giant crowd is silent as Ryder sits on a stool and sings from his heart. *"Baby, I never knew, not until you, the way I could feel, my soul you unpeel, like an onion, I'm not funnin' . . ."* The lyrics don't feel like they're coming through my ears and getting translated by my brain in the normal way; they're becoming part of me.

He stops in the center of the stage and looks straight out, his eyes dreamy. *"I like you, baby. At least I think so, maybe. No matter what they say, I won't go away, from now on it's just you and me, we're free-er . . . than . . . freeeeeeee!"* He looks into the camera and smiles—not one of his big, gleaming ones; it's a small, personal smile that feels like it's for me. The video stops. It's been two minutes and fifty-three seconds, but it feels like time stood still.

I think Madison says something to me, but I don't know for sure. I'm too busy staring into those eyes. At that smile.

"Uh-oh," Madison says, shaking her head. "I think you've landed."

Finally I'm able to look away from the frozen image of him on-screen. "Huh?"

"You've landed. You're a Lander. That's what Ryder's fans are called."

"Too bad we don't know how the love potion works," I tell her, only half joking. "We could use it on him."

"Oh my gosh, that would be unreal!" Madison squeals. Then she stops herself, like she's realized how far-fetched the idea is. "Yeah, the next time we see him, we'll have to do that." She laughs. "But right now, you have to help me papier-mâché his head."

Yuck. It's the last thing I want to do, but now that Madison's shared Ryder Landry with me, I owe her. So into the goop I go.

Blech!

3

I'm still in a happy state of Landryness when Dad and I take Toby for a walk. Men in T-shirts and women in tank tops are enjoying the almost-summer sunshine, jogging on the dirt path around the lake across from our house. I thought LA would get boring being sunny all the time, but in Ohio I might still be wearing mittens in May. I don't miss that at all.

An older man walks by quickly, reading a newspaper. Dad says hello and the man nods back. We see him every time we're out here. He's got a gray beard and really tan, leathery skin. It doesn't matter how warm or cold it is; he never wears a shirt and he's always in red shorts. He's like a neighborhood celebrity—to me, anyway. I've named him "Red Shorts," because I'm brilliant that way.

Toby sniffs and plays with some of the other dogs that pass by, and his favorite this afternoon is a nicely groomed golden retriever being walked by a lady with long legs in super-short shorts. She and Dad chat about how the dogs seem to like each other, and then she and her shiny pet walk in the other direction.

All the time I look for signs that Dad doesn't care about Terri anymore, but I never find any proof. Like just now, the lady with the dog was really pretty, but Dad didn't even notice. He still sometimes calls Terri his girlfriend until he corrects himself and says "ex," which sounds like the saddest syllable in the world. Dad and Terri weren't "hanging out" like Lisa Lee and Ronnie Cheseboro or Kylie Mae and Lonnie. Dad and Terri were in the kind of love that Ryder Landry sings about.

Ryder Landry. Those eyes. That smile. I can't wait to get back to my room and listen to more of his songs.

"Cleo! Why are you standing there? Come on!"

I look up and see Dad and Toby way ahead of me, about to cross the street. I didn't even realize I was standing in the path with people and dogs passing me as I stared into space thinking about Ryder Landry. Is this love?

No! I'm not in *love* with Ryder Landry. I think you need to *know* someone personally to love that person, but if Dad feels half of what I feel about Ryder right now, he needs to get back together with Terri.

"Coming!" I shout, and run to meet Dad.

Dad says it wasn't my fault he and Terri broke up. I don't agree, but it doesn't matter. It's my responsibility to get them back together. He was happy to see her at my play, but that was over three weeks ago—the night I got the love potion—and no matter what Focus! tries to teach me, sometimes I can't help being impatient. Dad is an old man—he might even be forty—and I don't want him to waste too much time. I ask him sometimes if he's talked to Terri, but he says she needs her "space." It seems to me like she has plenty of space, though, since she lives by herself at least two miles away from us.

Back home in my bedroom, I let Millie the millipede crawl on my hand as I kneel in front of my dresser. I stare at the little red bottle of love potion. It's only two or three inches tall, but to me it seems . . . powerful. Being careful not to knock Millie off my wrist, I pick up the bottle and take out its stopper.

I look inside. I swirl the liquid around, but it's kind of thick so it doesn't move much. I put my nose close to the opening and breathe in. If the potion has any smell, I can't tell, but that could be because Millie's terrarium is nearby, with some newly rotting fruit inside for him to eat.

I want to tip the bottle over, to feel the potion on my finger, maybe even taste it and see if it's sweet or sour or salty or nasty, but I stop myself.

Why hasn't Uncle Arnie told me how it works?

I look at my computer. I *could* just call him. I *have* called him before. He gave me advice about my voodoo doll when I needed it, and he congratulated me on the night of my play. Maybe he *wants* to hear from me. Maybe he's wondering why his little niece Cleo hasn't called in so long. All I need to do is push a couple of keys on the keyboard and I can find out everything I need to know.

But no. I promised myself I would wait for his instructions to come, like he said they would. I have willpower. I have focus. I can do it.

And I know one thing for sure: if I don't know how the love potion works, I definitely shouldn't play with it. Not as a joke at school, and not for Dad and Terri. Not yet.

But hopefully soon.

Having a love potion at home makes it hard to focus on things like storyboards and reading and chores. But it's equally hard back at school. Sixth grade is going to be over in three weeks (yay!), then it'll be my first summer in California. I can't wait to hang out with Madison all the time with no pressure of homework, or tests, or people like Lisa Lee and Kylie Mae around every day. I'm already picturing hot days in Madison's amazing backyard, sipping lemonade that Yvonne brings us, doing cannonballs into the pool, and listening to Ryder Landry music. Maybe I'll even learn to dance to it and not look like a dork. Yes, in my summertime fantasy, I'll dance like a glamorous gazelle, and when it gets dark, Madison's chef will make us dinner, and we'll watch Ryder Landry videos in her dad's movie room and read about Ryder on the Internet and have the best time ever. It'll be the most fantastic summer of my entire life!

I feel a tap on my shoulder. "Cleo," says Larry. "It's time to go to Focus!"

Of course I'm daydreaming when it's time to go to Focus! Whenever I'm not focusing, it's time for Focus! class.

Focus! used to have the reputation of being for dummies, but it feels a little different—sometimes even better—now. I think that's mainly because Larry was so good and funny in the *Healthyland* play, and he's a Focus! kid along with me.

"Look at the lovebirds! Aren't you going to hold hands while you walk to your class?" Ugh. It's Lisa Lee, chirping in her phony-sweet voice and batting her eyelashes.

"Cleo and Larry, sittin' in a tree," Kylie Mae adds, always following Lisa Lee's lead. I don't see her face because I'm already leaving the room, but I'm sure her cornflower-blue eyes are as empty and dull as always.

Dad tells me not to "hate" anything, but I can't help it; I hate when they do things like this. Larry is my friend, but I don't want anyone thinking I love him. I don't love anybody like that . . . except maybe Ryder Landry.

If Larry hears Lisa Lee and Kylie Mae, he pretends not to. "So what life-changing, mind-opening activity do you think Roberta will force on us today?" he asks as we walk across the courtyard.

I decide to forget about the nasty girls. "I think we'll learn how to build personal flying machines so we can fly ourselves to and from school," I say . . . because this is exactly the kind of excellent, useful thing we would never learn in Focus! Usually we play word games or goof around with toys that are supposed to teach us some kind of life lessons, but we're never really sure what.

And that's exactly what Roberta has in mind today. When we get to class, there are puzzle pieces waiting for us on each table. But they're not flat puzzles with pictures of scenery or kitty cats; these are three-dimensional blocks of different shapes and sizes.

"Hooray, puzzles," Larry comments sarcastically as he sits in the chair next to me. "Looks like we'll have to wait until next week to start designing the robots that will cook our food and do our homework."

Samantha takes a seat at the next table over. "I love puzzles," she says, staring blankly at the pile of blocks on her table. Her complete lack of enthusiasm makes Larry burst out laughing. Sam smiles too.

"Give me your focus, everybody! Focus!" Roberta shouts, clapping her hands. I wonder if she gets paid based on how many times she says "Focus!" in a day, because she says it a lot. "Today you're going to focus on . . ."

"Puzzles," Larry and Samantha say at the same time.

"Yes, puzzles," says Roberta. "But more than that. You'll see." She's going to place us in groups, and each of us will take a turn being the leader. For ten minutes the leader will make all of the decisions, and then we'll switch. It sounds like a silly way to spend thirty minutes of a school day, but hey, it's better than trying to roll my *r*'s in Spanish or stay awake during a movie about the Civil War.

Because Sam's closest, Roberta puts her with me and Larry. Great. Sam and I nod at each other. It's hard to believe that she was once the best friend I'd ever had. The only other person who came close was Jane Anne in Ohio, who I knew since I was a baby. She stopped talking to me in fifth grade and I never knew why. Then I moved away and didn't even get to say goodbye. I don't want that to happen with Sam. I don't want anyone else in my life to disappear without any explanation.

Larry looks back and forth at me and Sam saying nothing to each other. "Well, I've got two words for this situation!" he says in a booming voice. "Awk. Ward." Sam and I both let out quiet, nervous laughs. It will be nice if Larry's jokes keep this from becoming too weird.

"Cleo told me you were funny, Scab . . . Larry," Sam says. I breathe a mini sigh of relief because she stopped herself from calling him "Scabby Larry," which people have been doing since second grade, when someone supposedly saw him eat one of his scabs. "I guess she was right about something for once."

Ouch. Looks like Samantha's not ready to be friends yet.

Larry doesn't seem to notice Sam's meanness toward me. "Cleo said I was funny?" he says. "I've only heard her describe me as having genius smarts and crazy good looks."

"I did not!" I shout. "I never said—"

Before I even finish my sentence, Larry cuts me off. "My trademark sarcasm! Don't even think about stealing it. Now, who wants to be the leader first?"

We all look at each other. More silence. Awk. Ward.

"Cleo, you're first alphabetically. Why don't you go?" Larry suggests.

"*Great* idea," says Sam. I'm sure she wants to go first because she's really smart, but it took me a while to realize that she's also pretty bossy.

"Hey," Larry says in a jokey tone. "Remember, sarcasm is mine. Trademarked."

"Okay." Sam laughs, shooting Larry the biggest, warmest smile I've seen since she and I were friends. Then she turns to me, frowning. "I don't think that's the *best* idea ever, but go for it, Cleo."

Now that I'm under the pressure of Sam's unfriendly attitude, our three-dimensional puzzle tower gets off to a slow start. First I suggest we group the pieces with similar shapes together. Sam sighs, but we do it anyway. Then I change my mind and decide we should divide the pieces by size: small, medium, and large. "Aren't we supposed to be *building* this tower?" Sam asks, piling up the medium pieces.

"Not necessarily," Larry replies. "We're supposed to be following Cleo's lead. *That's* going to be today's lesson. Learning leadership skills."

Sam nods. "Aha! You are a smart one, Scab—uh, Larry! No matter what Cleo said."

I'm really happy they're getting along (Cleo's trademark sarcasm!) while my brain is working overtime trying to figure out how to start this puzzle. Sam doesn't want to wait anymore, though. She dives in and creates a base for the tower out of the large pieces. By the time Roberta tells us it's time for the next leader, Samantha has already taken charge, telling us exactly what to do. But when I start to put a blue L-shaped block on the tower the wrong way, she grabs it from me.

"I'll do it," she says, and places it perfectly. We get a lot of the tower done with Sam as the leader, but it's not much fun because I'm just quietly doing what she says.

When Larry is in charge, he asks our opinion of what should go next and we decide together. He places a piece, then I do, and then Sam does. Samantha compliments him on how quickly we're getting the project done, and it looks like he blushes a little. Even with all the embarrassing things we've had to do for the play or in Focus! class, I've never seen Larry blush.

When our tower is over a foot high, Larry picks up the last piece like it's the Olympic torch. "Today, my friends, we have built not only a ridiculous tower; we have built friendship and understanding." He pauses dramatically, raising the "torch" higher. "But only one of you can have the special privilege of placing the ultimate piece—"

Sam grabs it out of his hand and puts it on top. "There!" she says, slapping both hands on her hips and nodding in satisfaction.

I would be mad if Samantha ruined my moment (if I ever tried to create one), but Larry laughs. "Nice, Sam, taking charge!" Then they high-five!

What is going on here? I've never seen them get along like this. It almost seems like Samantha . . . *likes* him! And not in the way *I* like him. She's looking at him with dreamy sparkles in her eyes, like she's watching her first Ryder Landry music video. But this is *Larry.* One time not that long ago, Sam told me not to even be his friend. How could she go from thinking he was "Scabby Larry" to *liking* him so quickly? But I think she has!

"We did it!" Larry shouts, drumming his hands on the table. The tower shakes.

Sam drums too, yelling, "Earthquake!"

"Be careful!" I warn them. "It'll fall over!"

That only makes Larry and Samantha laugh and drum harder. "Who cares?" says Larry. "We still have the knowledge of a job well done, with three great leaders!"

"Well, two," Samantha cracks.

I'm too worried about our tower to even care. "It doesn't matter how well it's done if Roberta doesn't see it!" I try to stop them, but I only have two hands to their four, and . . . CRASH! The tower falls into what looks like a million pieces.

"Oh no!" I shout. Across the room, I see Roberta walking toward us. "Roberta, we were finished! Really, we were!"

"That's okay. I saw." Roberta knows we finished our tower and is happy we all learned about different styles of leadership. Larry and Sam scoop up the blocks and return them to the supply closet in the back of the Focus! room, laughing and chatting like old friends the whole time.

Old friends . . . or two people falling in love.

I'm starting to get an idea.

4

Like almost every day when Dad drives me home from school, I run to the house while he checks the mailbox. He usually grumbles that there's nothing but advertising and bills ("Wasting paper!" he says), but today his voice stops me before I reach the front door.

"Cleo! There's something here for you."

I turn around. Something in the mail can only mean one thing—Uncle Arnie! No one else has ever sent me anything.

I practically tackle Dad to the ground, grabbing at the pile of papers in his hand. "What is it? Which one? Where, where?"

He gives me his famous "calm down" look. It's so easy to spot, he should trademark it, like Larry with his sarcasm. So I put my hands by my sides and bite my bottom lip, but I still can't help bouncing around a little on my toes. And

Dad can't stop the voice inside my head from saying, *Come on, come on, come on!*

Finally, after what seems like a million years, he hands me a postcard and walks inside.

The side with the picture is facing up. It's actually two photos next to each other. One shows a cute little pink cottage with a white porch in front, and the other shows a room stuffed with books from floor to ceiling. The words in the corner of the card say "Maple Street Bookshop, New Orleans, Louisiana."

I turn the postcard over and immediately recognize the scrawl. It's the same writing from my voodoo doll instructions.

Knowledge is power, said somebody important. Blaze your own trail, said somebody else. Go, go, go, my friend Cleoooooo!

There's no signature.

Uncle Arnie for sure.

I turn it over again. What is he trying to say? Is he telling me a story? Giving me a clue to something? Is the meaning of life hidden here somewhere?

I look at the photos more carefully. There's an orange cat stretched out on the floor in front of the books, and an owl perched on the top bookshelf. But the owl's not real; it's wearing glasses and a hat with a tassel like it's graduating from high school.

"Cleo, time to start homework!" Dad's muffled voice is coming from inside the house, and suddenly I realize I'm still standing out on our front path.

I run inside, straight to my room, and carefully place the postcard on my dresser, standing it against my bottle of love potion. Are the two things related? They must be!

With all this in my head, I have a hard time working on my storyboards for the Immersive Interactive Art Installation. I sketch and sketch, but Pandaroo ends up flying around in space with a friendly, smart-looking owl, which isn't exciting at all. Storyboards are the building blocks of movies; they need to have action!

When Dad calls me for dinner, he asks to see the postcard, which I've brought to the table. "Don't get your messy vindaloo sauce on it," I warn him as I daintily hand it over.

"I'm not eating with my hands," he mumbles as he takes the postcard. He looks at the photos, then turns it over and reads the other side super quickly. He laughs and hands it back. "I think that's bacon," he says.

"No, it's chicken vindaloo."

"I mean the quote. 'Knowledge is power.'"

Dad is just as confusing and strange as Uncle Arnie! "If it's a quote, how can it be bacon?" I ask.

"No, Francis Bacon. A writer from the fifteen hundreds.

He might have been the first one to say it. But a lot of people have said it since."

"What about 'Blaze your own trail'?" I ask.

"Lots of people have said that too."

"So, what does it all mean?"

Dad finishes chewing, then shrugs. "What does your uncle Arnie ever mean?" He scoops up some rice with his fork, and I edge the postcard farther away from him. "I think it's up to you to decide."

After Dad says that, I really can't concentrate on homework. And I definitely have a hard time getting to sleep that night. As I stare at my ceiling in the darkness, I keep asking the same question: *Uncle Arnie, why are you so confusing?*

I fall asleep without an answer. But when I wake up, I'm bursting with a fantastic idea. I don't know where it came from, but I know it can be accomplished—today!— when we go on our school field trip to the Central Library in downtown Los Angeles.

All I need to do is find a book of love potions ("Knowledge is power!") and pick one that will make Larry and Samantha fall in love. Somehow in the middle of the night, I realized Uncle Arnie doesn't want me to wait for his instructions; he wants me to do it myself!

My heart is almost exploding with happiness because this is such an awesome, positive thing I can do for the girl who was once my best friend. She already likes Larry for sure. He seems to like her too. And even though sixth-grade boyfriends and girlfriends usually make me as sick as a bucket of lumpy papier-mâché does, I could accept those two as a couple . . . because they'd *both* be my friends then! If Sam is hanging out with Larry, she'll talk to me more and more, and eventually she'll be my friend again. I'll have the group I've always wanted.

Today I'll blaze my own trail, just like Uncle Arnie wrote. With Madison's help, I hope.

When it's time to go to the library, we get in a line and walk out to the school parking lot, where a big yellow school bus is waiting for us.

It feels like I'm going back in time as I climb up the stairs. The tall steps are just like the ones in Ohio; the seats are the same shade of green, with the same thin, uncomfortable padding. I've done this a million times, but for the kids in my class, it's a weird treat. They don't ride school buses; they've always been dropped off by parents and nannies and au pairs. "Oh my gosh, I feel like I'm in one of those old teen movies!" Madison says, looking around with the amazement I might feel if I were on an actual movie set. "Where should we sit?"

Finally I'm an expert at something! "The backseat," I say. "It's the bounciest, so it's the most fun, and we get to see everyone come on."

We sit down and watch as Lisa Lee and Kylie Mae walk

on together, with Ronnie and Lonnie Cheseboro behind them. "Weirdness! It's totally like in the movies!" Lisa Lee announces.

Madison looks at me and smiles. "I guess I still have some things in common with them," she says. Madison never totally stopped being friends with Lisa Lee and Kylie Mae; she just started having lunch and hanging out with me more often. They all still text sometimes and even do things on the weekends, but Madison doesn't tell me anything about it. So I don't ask.

The popular lovebirds hold up everyone else in line by standing in the middle of the bus and giggling about who's going to sit where, and whether the girls are going to sit with the boys or each other. Finally they decide that the boys will sit behind the girls. I can only imagine the teasing and poking and giggling that will follow. Ugh.

"Is this seat taken?" asks Larry, plopping down into the seat across from me and Madison without waiting for an answer. He stretches his legs out like he's going to take up the whole space, but when he sees Samantha looking around for a free seat, he shouts for her to come back toward us.

"Do you have room here?" she asks Larry. She almost seems shy—which is not normal for Samantha!

"Sure." Larry pulls his feet back and lets her sit down. "As long as you're not allergic to monkeys." He lifts his monkey figurine out of his backpack and holds it up.

"Oh, cute! I've been wanting to see this little guy close

up!" Sam is talking in a high-pitched, enthusiastic voice I've never heard before. Something is definitely up.

This is exactly why my love potion idea is so brilliant! Unfortunately, it's impossible to tell Madison my plan with Sam sitting two feet away, so instead I ask if she's read about Ryder Landry's tour of Asia this summer. Of course she has. It was on the *WickedHappyTeenTime* blog this morning. She also knows his favorite Asian food (Korean barbecue) and the color of the sleep mask he wears on long flights (blue).

"Are you a Lander, Cleo?"

Like most school buses in the world, this one is rickety and noisy, especially with windows open and horns honking and cars passing by. But I swear that question came from Sam on the other side of the aisle. I turn and see she's smiling.

"*You're* a Lander?" I ask.

"Yeah! I didn't think you knew who he was. Your dad listens to all those boring podcasts and old music."

"Madison told me all about him, and now I'm his biggest fan," I tell her.

"Except for me," Madison says.

Larry leans across Sam toward us. "Except for me!" he says.

We all look at him in silence. Ryder definitely has boy fans, but Larry is not the kind of boy who likes anything normal and popular.

"Okay, I'm lying," he says. "Actually, I can't think of a

human being I want to know less about. I built my little sister a whole fort out of pillows in our basement so she could sing his idiotic creepo-teen-robot tunes as far from my ears as possible."

"Well, that's too bad, Larry," says Sam, launching into some Ryder Landry lyrics—loudly! *"When I need to talk, or take that long, long walk, you're the one who won't say no."*

I recognize the song right away. I have a lot of favorites already, but it's one of my *favorite* favorites. Madison and I join in. *"Because you're my friend, my friend, my friend to the end of the Earth!"*

It's a little weird to be singing this song of deep and lasting friendship with my best friend and the girl who used to be my best friend, but it's ridiculously funny to see Larry plugging his ears with his fingers and howling like a coyote with a stomachache, so we keep going. Larry shouts and begs for us to stop . . . which we don't, until we arrive at the library.

That might have been the most fun bus ride I've had in my life.

5

'm so excited when we get to the library, I'm ready to explode . . . and it's not just because of my awesome plan—the plan I still haven't gotten to tell Madison. This library is actually a cool-looking place. It's not boxy and boring; it's like an old castle or fortress, with statues built into the building and a colorful mosaic pyramid on the top of a tower. Our teacher, Kevin, says it takes up the whole city block and houses a hundred bazillion books—or some big number. I'm not totally listening; I'm just hoping one of those books has love potions in it!

Kevin leads us into the big main room. It's got a super-high ceiling with chandeliers hanging down and a long desk with four librarians working behind it. Kevin hands out our library cards and says we're supposed to pick two books we'd like to read, and do a report on one at the end of the school year. He tells us to meet right back here in one hour, not a minute later. He reminds us to keep our voices low, to not talk to strangers (unless they work there), and to pair up and always stay with our buddy.

"I never leave my buddy's side," Ronnie Cheseboro says, draping his arm over Lisa Lee's shoulder.

"Ewww, gross," Lisa Lee says, squirming away, but I can tell she loves the attention.

Madison's my buddy; we don't even need to talk about it. She knows I have something important to discuss, and we've got eight floors to ourselves for the next hour. As we run to the elevator and the door closes, I spot Samantha and Larry walking up the stairs together, and she's laughing at everything he says.

I knew it! She likes him. All we need is a potion—*with* instructions—so they'll *both* fall in love. I explain it all to Madison in the elevator. "It's obvious that Samantha loves Larry, but if Larry loves her back, she'll have no choice but to become part of our group."

"Why's that important?"

That part's harder to explain, but I tell Madison the truth, even if it's slightly embarrassing. I tell her how uncomfortable I feel not being able to talk with Samantha, passing her in the lunchroom, and trying to avoid her in Kevin's classroom and in Focus! The fact is, I miss Sam as a friend.

"But we just had fun on the bus with her," Madison

points out as we head toward a computer we can use to search for books.

"Right! Because she was with Larry! Once we get them together for real, she'll be your friend, she'll be my friend, she'll be everybody's friend!" I must have shouted that last part because we get a "Shhh!" from a librarian behind a nearby desk. "Sorry," I whisper in her direction.

I lower my voice and turn to Madison, who's typing search words into the computer. "All we need is *the right book.*"

Madison lifts her hands off the computer keyboard and turns to me. "No books," she says, disappointed.

I'm not giving up yet. I need to blaze my own trail! "Come on, there are a million bazillion books here! Look up *spells*. Look up *charms*. Try another language, anything!" Madison's fingers fly across the keyboard. Then they stop. I peer over her shoulder to look at the screen. "Did you find something?"

"Glad you asked." Madison steps back from the computer and pushes me toward it. I read the title on the screen. Then I read it again. I'm confused. And she can tell.

"It's the only thing they have," she says.

I look at it again. It says:

¡POCIÓNES FANTÁSTICOS PARA LA VIDA Y AMOR! (Los hechizos y encantos

para encontrar el amor, mantener el amor, y
crean el amor que antes no existía)

Obviously it's in Spanish. I easily figure out POTIONS
FANTASTIC (the nouns and adjectives are backward in
Spanish), and the word *amor* again and again and again. I'm
hoping that means "love."

I can't translate it all, but I understand enough to know
that this book could change everything.

Now that we've found the listing for the book, we have
to find the book itself—which is not so easy in this gargan-
tuan library. First we have to figure out the floor, and we're
so busy jabbering in the elevator that we miss it, so we have
to go all the way to the top floor and then wait to go back
down again.

Finally we spot the room with the Spanish-language
books. As we run inside, we happily shout some of our
favorite Spanish words (*¡Hola! ¡Adios! ¡Feliz Navidad!*) and
are shushed by another librarian. Quieting down (but not
slowing down, not at all), we zoom up and down the aisles.
I've never seen so many *palabras de español* (words of Spanish) in my life! Shelves and shelves and shelves of words I
don't understand. Words like *etéreo, místico,* and *muertos vivi-
entes.* Luckily, the Dewey Decimal system is in numbers, not
Spanish, so we finally find *POCIÓNES FANTÁSTICOS.*

My hand is almost shaking as I pull it off the shelf. The

book is definitely old. The edges of the pages are thick, yellowish, and raggedy. The cover artwork is faded and lame-looking. It's just a simple drawing of a bottle—sort of like my bottle of love potion, but purple—with a hand lifting up its stopper so hearts and flowers can fly out. I could have designed something way more creative. Still, I'm holding this book like it's from ancient times, as if any page could turn to dust with the touch of my dirty fingertips.

Madison shakes me. "Let's look inside!"

I carefully open the book. There are illustrations inside on every couple of pages, but there are also lots and lots of words. "Wow," I say, overwhelmed. "It's *todo español*."

Madison nods. "It doesn't look easy."

"I guess we could pick a potion and I could . . . translate it," I offer, knowing I don't really want to, no matter how excited I am. I've got enough homework already.

"*You'll* translate?" If this were the Madison I used to know, I'd say she was being mean or judgey, but she's just joking because she knows I'm pretty slow at Spanish. *Muy despacio,* as a matter of fact. And that means *really slow*!

We sit on the floor with the book open between us. I concentrate for a minute and, to my surprise, I get an idea. "I know! I'll pick the pages that look the best and scan them on my dad's printer. Then I can email them to myself and translate them online."

"Perfect!" Madison says. "I was going to say Yvonne

could help me, but I don't need her telling my mom or dad that I'm translating love potions. They're already worried about how much I like Ryder Landry."

I stand up, ready for action. "Well, once Larry falls in love with Samantha, I want to use one on my dad and Terri. Then maybe you and Ryder can be next."

"Ha ha," Madison says. Suddenly there's a ringing noise from inside her backpack. She jumps back in surprise. "Oh no!"

"What is it?" I ask.

"I set my alarm for when we have two minutes left," she says.

"Two minutes? You couldn't have given us more time?"

She stares at me. "How much time did you set *your* phone for?"

Good point.

We haven't even looked for any other books, and we definitely don't want any from the Spanish-language section. We rush out of the room with *POCIÓNES FANTÁSTICOS*, shouting "*¡Gracias!*" at the librarian. We're gone so fast, we can barely hear her shush us.

We wait all of two seconds after pressing the elevator button, then scramble down the stairs instead. When we get to the first floor, we see Kevin in the distance, standing by the main desk. No one else is around him.

"You're late, ladies! Check out your books and let's go!"

"Grab anything!" Madison says, but I'm already doing

exactly that. I pick the thinnest book I can find off a random shelf. Perfect for a book report!

Madison and I toss our books on the desk. The librarians slide them over a scanner, and we cram them in our backpacks. Kevin leads us onto the crowded bus. As we look for seats, kids grumble about us being late. "What were they doing anyway?" Ronnie Cheseboro says to Lisa Lee.

"Madison was helping Cleo learn to read," she suggests, and they laugh.

I glare as I pass their seat and squeeze in with a kid I don't know. When the bus gets moving, I look around and see Larry and Sam still together—even now, when they don't have to be buddies! It will only take one small sip of love potion to push them into boyfriend-girlfriend land for sure.

I open my backpack. I touch the rough edges of the potion book, promising myself I'll translate something as soon as I can. Then I pull out my other book. I'm hoping it will be easy to read, but I'm not that lucky.

Quantum Physics, Biocentrism, and the Universe as We Know It.

That sounds like a lot of stuff for a little book.

I'm going to have to work out a deal with Kevin. I'll start on that after he gets over us being late for the bus.

After school, instead of doing homework, I lie on my bed with *POCIÓNES FANTÁSTICOS* and try to pick my favorite potion. Since I only know a few of the words, I do my judging by looking at the drawings. They're all so lame and basic: men's and women's faces with hearts in between them, bottles that look like they hold potion, cups you might drink from, jewelry, scenery, and even toys. (I decide right away to avoid anything that looks even close to a voodoo doll.) I read some of the Spanish words aloud, as if saying them could help me figure out what they mean.

I'm mumbling to myself *en español* when Dad knocks on my door and walks right in before I can even tell him to wait.

"Dad!" I shout, slamming the book shut and turning it over so he doesn't see the title. He doesn't know Spanish, but he might be able to figure it out.

"Oh, good, I'm glad you're doing your homework," he says, then tells me he's going to take Toby on a jog around the lake. I'm glad, because since Terri broke up with him, he hasn't gone on any hikes or ridden his bike or even walked very fast. But I'm even gladder because this will leave me alone for a while—with his computers!

I follow Dad to the front door and send him off with an overly happy wave. "Have an awesome time! Say hi to Red Shorts!" Dad looks confused by my enthusiasm, but Toby barks happily like he agrees.

Once I see them turn down the dirt path that circles the lake, I run to the dining room and sit down in front of Dad's biggest computer. As long as I keep his piles of folders and junk and wadded-up papers in the places where he left them, he'll never know I was there. I carefully use one of his printers to scan my favorite-looking potion so far—the one called *COSAS DULCES PARA TU DULCE CORAZÓN*.

Judging by the pictures, it looks like you have to cook a bunch of ingredients in a pot on a stove. Until recently, Dad only trusted my cooking skills with the microwave, but lately he's let me be more independent. Not only will he leave me alone, like today, he also lets me boil water and make sure the oven is preheated properly.

Once the potion recipe pops up on his computer, I email it to myself, then erase the evidence that I was ever there. On the computer in my room, I copy the recipe into a translation program, and a few seconds later it's in English— though some of it is a little off.

The potion is called STUFFS SWEET FOR YOUR HEART SWEET.

I guess the translator who created the program forgot the adjectives-before-nouns rule in English.

Start with a pot sturdy on stove hot. Make water boil gently. Melt chocolate tasty and strawberry ripe to create a mixture bold. Add seven drops of honey sweet. Stir several times. Breathe in the aroma. Delicious, no? But wait! This is not enough to make a person of interest love you. We must be realistic. Love is not always sweet!

Love is full of surprises strange! Another flavor
unexpected must be added. Chop onion and
crush into pieces small. Add to liquid for a surprise zesty. Even a fool cannot prove it wrong.
It is foolproof! Foolproof, I say with vehemence!

That makes me laugh. And though there's no one here
to appreciate how strong I've been, I sit back and nod, proud
of myself for blazing my own trail and not being tempted
to use Uncle Arnie's love potion. Then I read the final paragraph of the potion I figured out myself.

Once cooled, put mixture in container. When
time is perfect, place three drops into a drink of
the person you desire. The next person to whom
he (or she) speaks ten words is the person with
whom he (or she) will fall in love indeed. Let us
hope that will be you!

I type a sentence in English into the translator just to
see how it comes out. In Spanish it's *Espero que no me va a ser.*
I hope it *won't* be me!

6

"Who knows what chemistry is?" Kevin asks the next morning as we start science class.

Hearing the word *chemistry,* Madison turns to me and smiles big, her straight white teeth sparkling. She's thinking about the same thing I am. It's the Ryder Landry song we love, "Chemistry Class"—"*You, you, you plus me, me, me. Put us together, it's chemistry. It's a reaction, an attraction, put us together and there's plenty of action!*"

Larry raises his hand, but as usual he doesn't wait to be called on. "It's when you get to blow things up!"

Kevin raises his voice over our laughter. "As is often the case, Larry is partially correct. That is *one* of the things that happen in chemistry. Remember earlier in the year, when Larry taught us about matter?"

I do. Even though Larry wasn't my friend yet, I liked his presentation on Albert Einstein, the wacky-looking super-smart scientist with fuzzy hair like my uncle Arnie's. Kevin tells us that chemistry is the study of how matter (which Albert Einstein discovered or named or something) is put together and how it can change.

Lonnie Cheseboro makes a snoring sound, and Kylie Mae giggles. At least Lonnie's paying attention. Ronnie is wadding up little bits of paper and tossing them into Lisa Lee's hair as she stares out the window.

Kevin ignores the snore and continues. "Chemistry is a lot more exciting than it sounds because, as Larry pointed out, sometimes these atoms—the building blocks of matter—come together and explosions occur."

A couple of people whoop with excitement. I'm still thinking, *It's a reaction, an attraction, put us together and there's plenty of action,* as Kevin continues. "Before there are any explosions, though," he says, "push your desks together and sit with the partners you had for our biology section."

Desks screech and scrape as they're pushed around the room. I was happy to be paired with Larry a couple of weeks ago for biology . . . though I wasn't quite so happy that Madison ended up with her old pal Lisa Lee. Dad once told me that jealousy is called a green-eyed monster, and I know why. As I see Madison and Lisa Lee chatting and looking friendly right now, I feel like my teeth and nails are getting sharper and that I could growl in their direction. I don't know why I'd have green eyes, though. I'll have to ask Dad sometime.

I snap out of my monster-like feeling when Larry does a jokey dance step as he trots toward me, holding his monkey toy up in the air and almost singing. "Mono—says 'oh no'— I'm gonna sit by Cleo!" He flops into the seat next to me and deposits the monkey on my desk. I pat it on the head and say hello.

"Aww, Cleo loves a monkey!" Lisa Lee says in a fake sweet voice. "And his name is Scabby Larry!" Kylie Mae reaches back from her desk and they smack hands. At least Madison swats at Lisa Lee a little. I just wish she'd looked a tiny bit more upset about it.

"Okay, everyone, calm down and settle in," Kevin says in a voice raised over the activity. "Now, Larry talked about blowing things up. . . ."

"And that's what we're gonna do!" Ronnie Cheseboro shouts, then high-fives his brother.

"Not exactly," Kevin says, "but I'll start us off with a simple demonstration." He lays a towel across his desk, sets down a two-liter bottle of soda, and opens the top. He puts a plastic funnel into it, then holds up a handful of small, round white things. "These are simple mint candies. I'm going to put them in the soda all at once through the funnel, and watch what happens when these two types of matter meet."

I'm no scientific genius but I'm one step ahead of Kevin. When you mix soda and mints, I bet there's *a reaction, an attraction, put them together and there's plenty of action!*

Kevin drops the mints into the soda, and WHOOSH! There's a reaction all right. Foamy soda sprays up and out of the bottle, making a big mess on Kevin's desk and even spilling onto the floor. Some of the kids in the front row are afraid of being hit, so they run from their desks. It's awesome!

I've decided I like chemistry. Not only does Ryder Landry find it interesting enough to write about, it also makes a mess in the classroom. Now I'm hoping my first chemistry experiment with Madison—our love potion— will work just as well!

I've figured out the perfect time to make it happen: at the Immersive Interactive Art Installation, which is Friday— only three nights away. That means a *poción fantástico* has to be made . . . and soon.

I convince Dad that Madison and I need a "study afternoon" to help each other finish our projects. I've been very secretive about my storyboards, so he doesn't know I'm already finished—ahead of schedule! The only thing I need to do is pick the best one to display. It's important to choose wisely because it's not only for the school; it'll also be seen by Hollywood producers, like Madison's dad. Maybe he'll be so impressed that he'll hire me to work on his next outer space blockbuster. Then I'll get Ryder Landry to do a song for it and I'll make Lisa Lee and Kylie Mae pay hundreds of dollars to go to the premiere!

I know it's a crazy fantasy, but considering I'm about to concoct a love potion to make my boy-who's-a-friend (not boyfriend) fall in love with my former best friend, why not keep an open mind?

Madison comes home with me and Dad after school, and on the ride I convince Dad to go out to his favorite coffeehouse. That will take much longer than a jog around the lake with Toby. As a treat I tell Dad I'll make dinner. I figure if we're going to be working on the stove anyway, I could heat up some soup too.

"Okay, I'll be gone about an hour," he says, putting his green messenger bag over his shoulder. "Actually, maybe an hour and a half. I think I'll take my bike instead of driving."

"That sounds great, Dad!" I tell him. "Take all the time you want."

He says goodbye, but I don't even see him leave because Madison and I are already running down the hall to my bedroom.

POCIÓNES FANTÁSTICOS is a strange-looking book that Dad would definitely notice in my room, so I hid it in the same dusty place I once hid my voodoo doll—under my bed. I shimmy underneath to get it, and when I slide back out and turn around, I'm face to face with a big, bright orange . . . human head!

Okay, it's not a head exactly, but it's *shaped* like a head. Sort of. The top is smooth and round like an egg, but there's a small point in the middle—a nose, I suppose—and something that kind of looks like a chin at the bottom.

This must be the latest version of Ryder Landry!

Of course, Madison couldn't capture Ryder's smooth, flawless skin, since she's used ripped-up pieces of paper and that pasty goop, but she painted his newspaper "skin" a color that looks like he's been in a tanning bed too long. His eyes are bright blue, but his eyelashes are big and thick and girly. Madison must have borrowed some fake ones from her mom.

"Do you like it?" she asks.

I hold my breath to keep from laughing.

"Yeah, it's . . . beaut—" But I can't even get to "iful" without starting to laugh.

"Well, it's not *done,* duh!"

I take a drink from a bottle of water and almost choke on it. "I'm sorry, he's gorgeous, he's handsome; I can't tell the difference between this and the real thing!"

"You like him? For real?"

I look at the orange newspaper skin and the bald head, and I do what any good friend would do. I lie my butt off.

"Of course I like him. I love him!"

"Oh, you *loooooove* him?" Madison asks. "Like Lisa Lee loves Ronnie Cheseboro?"

"More!" I joke.

"Well, if you love him so much, you should kiss him!" She puffs up her lips, making smoochy sounds. "Come on, Cleo, kiss your boyfriend!" She turns Ryder's head so he's looking at me and moves it forward, inch by inch. I gaze at Ryder's way-too-pink painted lips, getting closer and closer to mine, as Madison sings one of our favorite Ryder songs: *"Then it'll be you and me, forever we'll be, sailing on a boat on the sea of love . . ."*

I close my mouth tightly and jump up on my bed. "No, I can't! I won't!"

Madison lifts the Ryder head toward me, still singing. *"In a boat—sunshine all the time—in a boat—seagulls, foam, and brine . . ."*

"No más!" I say jokingly in Spanish. I put my hands over my mouth, then mumble through my fingers, "Come on, we need to get serious"—which makes us both burst out laughing.

Madison gives up and lowers the head. "Okay, let's go."

"To the kitchen!" I announce, jumping off the bed.

"Wait!" Madison shouts before I get through the door. I stop and turn around.

She's standing in front of my dresser, gazing at the little red bottle of love potion. Ryder's ridiculously blue eyes seem to be staring at it too. "What about this?" she asks.

"What about what?" I say, though I know exactly what she's thinking. Of course she wants to use Uncle Arnie's love potion. Who wouldn't?

Madison puts Ryder's head on the dresser and picks up the bottle. "Maybe we could just put one little, teeny drop in. How bad could that be?"

I sigh. "It could be *really* bad," I tell her. "Don't you remember farting like a mule when you talked in Focus! class? Remember cursing like crazy and getting expelled?" I feel like a party pooper who doesn't like having any fun, but it has to be said. "That was all because Sam and I used magic we didn't understand."

"Well, we don't know if that's really true—" Madison begins, but I cut her off.

"*I* believe it," I tell her. "And I promised myself I wouldn't use the potion until Uncle Arnie tells me how it works. I need to do it that way." I surprise myself with how serious I sound. "I *have* to do it that way."

Madison sighs and turns the Ryder head toward her face. "What do you think, Ryder?" she asks. After a moment, she turns to me. "He says it's okay. But only because it's . . . *you and me, forever we'll be, sailing on a boat on the sea of love . . .*"

We run out the door. "*In a boat—sunshine all the time—in a boat—seagulls, foam, and brine . . .*" By the time we've finished another verse, we're in the kitchen and ready to go.

Madison places Ryder's head on the kitchen table "so he can watch the action," and we open the cabinet underneath the sink. Most of our pots are severely scratched up, with rust or burnt patches of black on the bottom. Finally I spot a larger pot (a "sturdy" one, like the recipe calls for), which looks shiny and almost new.

I put the pot on the stove and turn the left front knob. It clicks a couple of times, and I know to stand back because Dad taught me that sometimes the flames burst out a little bigger than you expect. When the clicking stops, there's a quiet POOF sound, and flames erupt below the pot. I plan to turn them down, but Madison distracts me by asking, "Where do you guys keep the chocolate?"

She's already got her head in our refrigerator, scoping out the strawberry jam, which we decided to use since our strawberries look a little brown and hairy. "I'll get it," I say, sliding our step stool over and reaching for the powdered chocolate we put in our milk. It's on a high shelf with the honey bear Dad uses for his tea.

"Ow, it's already hot!" Madison shouts. I turn to see her pulling her hand away from the pot's handle.

Shoot, I meant to put water in there first! I run over to look at the pot. The bottom's getting black. I doubt Dad will ever notice, but I still rush to fill a glass with water and I toss it in the pot. It sizzles loudly and even spits a little, making us both jump back. "Why don't you scoop some of the jam in there while I grab the chocolate?" I tell Madison. "But be careful; that pot sounds angry!"

"Well, that's no way to start a love potion," she says to the pot, spooning jam into it. "You be nice."

I've got both the chocolate and honey in my hands when Toby squeezes through his dog door, galloping toward me and leaping up like he wants to give me a hug. I lose my balance and jump off the stool. One second later, the tin of chocolate hits the ground and explodes in a big puff of brown powder. "Oh no!" Madison cries. Of course, I didn't drop the honey bear, because it's plenty sticky on the outside.

I take in the damage. Powdered chocolate is all over the floor *and* Toby. I brush some off him and drop to the ground to start scooping it up. "Is there any left?" Madison asks.

I pick the tin up off the floor, and luckily there's still some powder in the bottom. I join Madison near the pot. The strawberry jam has mixed with the water and is bubbling furiously.

Madison squeezes seven drops of honey into the pot; then I dump in the remaining chocolate. You'd think strawberry, chocolate, and honey would be a good combination, but this smells . . . nothing but wrong.

"I'll add some more water and stir," Madison says. "You get the onion."

I open the fridge, wishing the recipe had any vegetable but onion in it. Onions smell worse than farts, and you never get the smell off your fingers, and they make you cry if you don't cut them the right way, which I don't know how to do. I carefully cut a small chunk, hoping Dad doesn't notice, since it's the only onion we have. Then I cut the chunk into smaller pieces, tears coming to my eyes.

"Is that onion ready?" Madison asks. "This is getting kinda messy over here." Sure enough, our potion has become an unattractive brown substance that is bubbling up toward the edges of the pot. I should have kept an eye on it myself, but the stupid onion distracted me. One more reason to hate onions. Or, as Dad would make me say, *dislike them intensely.*

Madison stands back as I sprinkle a few small onion bits into the mess below. I take over stirring for a couple of seconds, then turn off the burner. "I think that's as good as it's gonna get," I say.

"Which is not good at all," Madison comments with a gaggy look on her face.

Together we pour—well, sort of *scrape*—the STUFFS SWEET into a coffee cup that we'll hide under my bed until the art show. Madison takes it to my room, the Ryder head under her arm, while I run hot water in the pot. But no amount of soaking or scrubbing is going to clean this pot. Its edges are forever stained with hardened strawberry-chocolate-honey-onion gunk.

I walk out of the kitchen, where Madison stops me in the doorway with a grim look. "We've got a problem," she says.

Her tone worries me. "What?"

She steps away from the doorway and lets me through to the hall, where I see Toby sitting and panting with his tongue hanging out . . . and chocolate all over his paws.

I was so busy with the recipe, I didn't notice that when

he ran out of the kitchen on his chocolatey paws, he decided to take a tour of the dining room . . . the living room . . . the hallway . . . my bedroom . . . and Dad's room!

Then I look out the kitchen window and see Toby safely running around in the backyard. *Now* he decides to go outside! I cover up his dog door with a chair so he can't get back in, and I wonder what else could go wrong.

At that moment, my phone dings. It's a text from Dad:

Heading home in 10–15 minutes. Hope you're cooking something good for dinner!

Even worse, he sent it over five minutes ago.

7

"Okay, we've got to work fast," I say to Madison. "Let's not worry about my bedroom. I can throw clothes and stuff on the ground and cover that up for a while."

"Or forever," Madison says.

"This is no time to joke!" This is a lie, because I'm actually laughing.

"I could vacuum your dad's room while you sweep the floors," Madison offers.

"You know how to vacuum?" I exclaim. Madison shrugs, embarrassed. Hey, if I had a maid, I wouldn't either. "You sweep, I'll vacuum," I tell her. Even if Madison's never swept a floor before, she can probably figure out how.

I direct Madison to the broom in the laundry room while I rush to our hall closet and grab the vacuum. Before Focus! class, I might have been paralyzed, too scared to make any decisions, but now I know how to "assess an emergency situation" and take charge. A few other items fall out of the closet with the vacuum, but I can't worry about those now. I run into Dad's room and plug in the vacuum. It comes to life with a loud VROOOOOOM. I run it over the beige carpet, but the brown chocolate stays right where it is.

I stop and look at the front of the machine. There's a clear-colored bin in the middle, but it's gray and gross, filled with dirt, hair, Toby fur, and every other disgusting thing that's come out of our carpets for who knows how long.

I pull out the icky bin, and some of the grossness flows over the side and onto the floor. In my head I see Dad already out of the coffeehouse, on his bike with his messenger bag over his shoulder, getting closer to our house with every second.

I assess the emergency situation again. I run to my room and dump the dirt in my trash can, where Dad won't notice; then I run back, pop the bin in, and start vacuuming. It works!

I can only hope Madison has taught herself to sweep.

When the carpet in Dad's room is clean, I unplug the vacuum and turn to push it back toward the hall closet. But something is blocking my way.

Dad.

Taking off his bike helmet, he says, "I think I've stepped into an alternate universe."

I don't know what to say to that except "Huh?"

He looks happy—he usually is after a large iced Americano with caffeine—so he must not suspect what's been going on. How could he? "Madison's sweeping, you're vacuuming. I thought you were going to make me dinner; I didn't know you were going to clean the house too."

"Yeah!" I say, putting the vacuum back in the hall closet with the other junk that fell out. "Madison and I got done with our stuff quicker than we thought, so we decided we'd tidy up."

I told a lot of lies when Samantha and I were doing our voodoo—too many—but I don't know if I've ever told one as big as this before! When have two kids ever, in the history of the world, chosen to vacuum and sweep?

"Well, that's awfully nice," Dad says. "Did you start dinner too?"

Oh no, he's heading toward the kitchen! Where the burnt pot is still in the sink!

"No, not really." I run ahead of him. "We tried something but then got busy with the cleaning, and . . . *Madison, my dad is asking what I'm making him for dinner!*" I shout, putting extra emphasis on *dinner* and hoping she gets the hint. I beat Dad to the kitchen, where Madison is sweeping the last of the chocolate into a dustpan. My eyes immediately dart to the sink.

The pot is gone!

"Where's . . . ?" I ask, mouthing *the pot* to Madison. She nods toward the trash can right as Dad walks into the kitchen. He breathes in, and his caffeinated smile goes away.

"It smells . . . interesting in here," he says.

"Oh, we were . . . um . . . experimenting with something for dinner, but it wasn't any good," I tell him as I run for the trash can. The burnt pot is sitting right on top, with the empty chocolate tin next to it. I pull out the plastic trash bag and tighten it up.

"Taking out the trash too? This must be my lucky day."

"It sure is, Dad!" I say. And when I think of the love potion in the coffee cup in my room, I realize that may actually be the truth—because if the love potion works for Samantha and Larry, Dad will be the next one to try it out. Then he'll be one step closer to getting back together with Terri.

I think I could be the best daughter of all time. He just doesn't know it yet.

On Friday morning, I choose my favorite storyboard for the Immersive Interactive Art Installation—the sequence of pictures featuring Pandaroo and Skunkifer in an action-packed outer space battle. Skunkifer, the evil villain who once had blond hair like Madison but now looks more like Lisa Lee, has kidnapped the Millipede with Many Shoes and hidden him in her lair filled with blue cheese, garlic, and other stinky stuff. (Our experience with the love potion recipe inspired me to add a few onions at the last minute.) Then Pandaroo rescues the grateful and relieved millipede from the skunk's clutches after a battle of cleverness and gymnastics, not violence. When I hand the storyboard to Kevin on Friday morning, I make a wish to get a good and prominent position in the Friendship Community Immersive Interactive Art Gallery (actually the gym) that night.

When Madison gets to class, she gives Kevin a big bag from a store called Hervé Léger. I know Ryder's head is inside. Considering how it still looked a little frightening the other afternoon, I hope she's had time to work on it since then!

Before Dad and I leave for the art show that night, there's a mega-super-important task I have to do: figure out how to transport the STUFFS SWEET to the event! I go into the bathroom, where Dad's medicine cabinet is filled with almost-empty bottles of cold medicine and cans of shaving cream with rust on the edges. I rummage around a bit, and on a shelf behind some hotel shampoos and conditioners I find what I was hoping for: eyedrops! The bottle looks pretty old and dusty, so I don't think Dad will miss it. It's got a squeezy black top that fills a little glass straw with liquid. I empty and wash it, then take it into my bedroom and pour our STUFFS SWEET potion into it. The potion's gotten thicker and gloppier and maybe even browner, but it's still liquid at least. Naturally, I spill some onto my desk as it makes its way from the big coffee cup into the tiny eyedrops bottle, but I can clean it up later. What's most important is that there are enough drops to make Larry and Samantha fall in love.

Dad shouts for me to meet him in the car in two minutes, but a flash of something sparkly grabs my attention. There, on my dresser, sits the red bottle of love potion. It looks extra glittery and pretty tonight, like it *wants* me to look at it. Like it's calling out, *"Use me! Use me!"*

Of course that's the potion we *should* be using. I know it's not in the *POCIÓNES* book, and we don't know exactly how it works, but Uncle Arnie's potion would be sure to give ours an extra boost. Just a drop couldn't hurt, could it?

I'm doing it.

I pick up the potion and open the top. I hold the eyedropper steady on my dresser and slowly tip the red bottle. I don't want too much to come out. I take a deep breath and tip the bottle just a little, little bit further. Then—

"One minute!" Dad yells from down the hall.

I stop.

What am I doing? I promised myself I wouldn't use Uncle Arnie's love potion without instructions. It's like he's testing me, sending postcards instead of the information I need. This is a cruel thing to do to a kid—especially an impatient one like me!

It's time to call him. Who knows whether a recipe from an ancient book written in Spanish is going to work or not? STUFFS SWEET might be a *poción fantástico,* or it might be a crock! Tonight's the night I need Uncle Arnie's magic. For good or bad, I know his magic works.

I push the button to start my computer. I told myself I wouldn't, but I really need to know.

"Thirty seconds and the car is leaving!" Dad yells. "I mean it."

My computer screen comes on. But thirty seconds isn't enough time. No matter how much I want to, I can't use Uncle Arnie's potion tonight.

I put the tops on both bottles, leaving Uncle Arnie's behind and putting the extra-special potion-filled eyedropper in the pocket of my jacket.

I did it. It was tough, but I showed willpower and focus and patience. I wish there were someone here to praise me. Unfortunately, it's just Millie the Millipede, and he's staying quiet.

I join Dad in the car—with almost five seconds to spare. "This is an exciting night, huh?" he asks as we're driving to school. I don't really care to make conversation, because I'm focused on everything that could happen tonight. So I reply with a simple "Yeah."

"You're awfully quiet. What's up?"

Of course, Dad doesn't know anything unusual might be happening at the art show; I'm sure he doesn't, but I immediately pull my hand out of my jacket pocket anyway, like the STUFFS SWEET has turned into lava. "Nothing!" I say. Luckily, he doesn't ask again.

The school parking lot is busy, full of kids and parents walking toward the gym, which is not just a big empty room anymore. The Immersive Interactive Art Gallery is hopping! It was a project for the seventh graders to create the décor for the event, and they did a great job. It looks like a cross between a hip Hollywood club and an art gallery. There are "walls" made of curtains, creating separate "rooms" for different types of art. Some areas have bright lighting, others are dim; one has a red light, and one little space even has a disco ball making patterns all around. Electronica music fills the whole space.

I walk ahead of Dad to the DJ booth (really a folding table), where Larry is sitting with big headphones over his ears. He's spinning old-fashioned records on an old-fashioned record player as he fiddles with music on his phone. His little carved monkey sits nearby, watching the action. Not wanting to disturb Larry's concentration, I just wave, but he slides off one of the headphones. "Hey, Cleo!" he says. "Like my art?"

"Playing music is your art project?" I ask. He nods with a smile.

"Very cool!" says Dad. I cringe. The word *cool* coming from an adult has the exact opposite effect. Dad introduces himself to Larry (even less cool!) and says he remembers him from our *Healthyland* play.

"Yeah, I can't believe a talent scout hasn't snapped me up yet, after my brilliant portrayal of Old King Kale," Larry says. Dad laughs way too loud, and I'm glad Larry has to change a record so I can drag Dad away to look for my storyboard.

I'm also looking for Ryder Landry's head, or Madison's—whichever comes first. But before I find either, I see a puff of yellow hair at the top of a stick-figure lady in high heels. It's Mrs. Paddington, with a not-super-real smile plastered on her face, standing next to Madison's father, who's texting on his phone.

"Look around, Dad," I say, running off toward Madison's parents without saying goodbye. "I need to find Madison!" Normally, I don't like to have conversations with the Paddingtons because they're not very nice, but tonight I dive right in. "Hi! How are you doing?" I ask, not waiting for an answer. "Where's Madison?"

Maybe it's my imagination, but Henry Paddington is looking at me like something he'd scrape off his shoe. At least Heather Paddington forces a smile. "She went to look for that . . . *head* she made," she says.

"Thanks! Have a great night!" I say, though I really don't care what kind of night they have. Madison is here and we have stuff to do! I jet off. But a few moments later, I stop fast, my sneakers squeaking.

At the front door, I see a flash of long red hair against the purpley-pink sky outside. It looks familiar, but I don't know how it could be . . .

"Terri?" I shout. The hair moves and a face looks toward me. It *is* her! I run over, wanting to give her a hug, but I'm not sure if it's appropriate to hug your dad's girlfriend when she's an ex. "What are you doing here?" I ask, trying to hide my excitement but failing, I'm sure.

She waits a second before she answers, like she's thinking of what to say. "I got invited by . . . um . . . one of the parents," she tells me. "They heard I work in graphic design and suggested I check out the artwork tonight. And of course I want to see yours."

"That'd be great! I'd love that!" I stop myself. I shouldn't be using words like *love,* especially with Dad and Terri in the same place and a love potion in my pocket!

"Hey, my dad's here," I tell Terri, though that's probably obvious. "Want to say hi?"

"Sure," she says, "but I'm going to look around a bit first."

"That's cool," I say, trying to beat down my usual over-enthusiasm. "We'll see you around."

Terri laughs. "You definitely will."

She's only a few steps away when I feel a tap on my shoulder. "Was that who I think it was?" Madison asks.

My hands are so moist and clammy I have to wipe them on my jeans. "Yes!" I say. "Terri is here and Dad is here, and here I am with . . . you-know-what." I wrap my hand around the eyedropper to make sure nothing has happened to it in the last few minutes. Nope, it's still there, ready for action.

"We may have more to do than we thought tonight," Madison says. "And I've figured out where we can start." She grabs my arm and pulls me to a corner of the gym, pointing me toward something that would be boring and normal on any other night in history. But tonight, it's exciting beyond belief.

The refreshments table! There are plates of cookies and trays of cheese and crackers, but most important, there are two big bowls—one of lemonade and one of red-colored punch. Drinks! Perfect for dissolving and distributing STUFFS SWEET FOR YOUR HEART SWEET.

The refreshments table: where the adventure begins.

8

"So, what do you think?" Madison asks. "A few drops in each bowl and let's see what happens! The school would go crazy!"

While I agree that would be hilarious, I know what can go wrong when you're not specific enough with magic, and I don't want anything like *that* to happen again! We need to concentrate only on the people we've discussed. Madison is a little disappointed, but she understands. "One of us could probably get Sam or Larry to drink something," I tell Madison. "But we have to make sure they're close enough to each other that the next person one of them says ten words to is the other one."

I have to take a breath. Boy, this is complicated! But I'm glad I figured it out on my own. "Maybe we should try Sam first," I suggest.

"Good idea! I could push Larry into her."

"Great!" I say. "Then she'd probably say something like, *'What the heck are you doing?'*"

Madison does some silent counting on her fingers. "That's six words."

I try another option, pretending to be Sam again. "Maybe, *'Watch where you're going, dork-ball!'*" That seems like an insult Samantha might use.

"Five words," Madison says. "Unless *dork-ball* is two."

"Maybe you push Larry hard enough into her that she spills her drink," I suggest. "Then she'd be more mad and say something like, *'Argh, you spilled my drink all over me, you ridiculous, lame-o dork-ball!'*"

"I think that's more than ten," Madison says. "I don't feel like counting."

I don't either. It's time to get to work.

I glance around the gym like an undercover spy sharing information with an informant on a train. Madison grins, her eyes sparkling with excitement. She starts to dip some lemonade into a plastic cup, but I stop her. Sam will like a red-colored drink better.

"Okay, cover me," I instruct Madison as I carefully pull the bottle from my pocket and unscrew the top. Feeling like a nurse taking blood from a patient, I squeeze the dropper and see it fill with our thick, dark concoction. My hand is shaking a little as I lift the dropper over the plastic cup with the punch in it. I give Madison a nod, and she gives one back.

Squeeeeeeze.

PLOP!

After two more squeezes I speedily put the top back on the potion, hiding it deep in my pocket. Then Madison and I both look down into the cup. Our love potion is not dissolving. It looks like three small brown jellybeans enjoying a swim.

"Are there straws?" I ask. We both look around the table and quickly realize there aren't. "Oh well, only one thing to do." I sigh.

I stick my finger in the punch and give it a gentle swirl. The blobs of love potion only break up a little, so I give it a less gentle swirl. When I'm finished, the red liquid has a brownish tint, but luckily it's inside a blue cup and hopefully Samantha won't look down at it before she drinks.

I pick up the cup, and Madison and I turn around to find Samantha.

"What did you just do?" A voice pierces through the electronica and the conversations.

It's Sam! And Larry isn't anywhere nearby!

I can't think of anything to say. The first semi-intelligent sound I make is "Hmmm?"

"What do you mean?" Madison says. Not brilliant either, but a little better than me.

"I saw you put something in that drink."

"Oh, that!" says Madison.

"Well, that doesn't sound nice at all for the lambs."

Kylie Mae steps in front of Lisa Lee, maybe protecting her from me. "Lambskin is *very* soft," she insists. "And it's very expensive to clean!"

"Look, I'm really, really sorry," I say. "I love your lamb coat and I didn't mean it any harm. For real. But I've got to go." I rush away, hearing one more comment from Kylie Mae as I go.

"She didn't even know what suede is! So lame!"

I almost laugh out loud. I've finally found the topic that will make Kylie Mae use her vocal cords: suede.

I turn a corner, hoping to find the aisle featuring Ryder Landry's head and Samantha's junk-and-flower sculpture of society, but I end up in the aisle of drawings and paintings . . . including mine.

I've been excited to see my storyboards on display, but now it's barely the third-most important thing on my mind.

Dad and Terri are right there. Standing together. Pointing at the artwork and talking. Looking nice. Looking friendly. Looking . . . right together.

And here I am, with a cup full of love potion!

Sure, it's meant for Sam, but Madison has an extra cup for that.

This is fate. This is meant to be. Isn't that what people always say about love?

I'm going to make this happen while I can.

I run up to them, making sure not to spill the punch. "Dad! You found Terri!"

"Actually, she found me," he says.

"Cleo, your storyboard is great!" Terri says. That's nice to hear, especially from a professional in the graphic arts business, so I take a look. Pandaroo seems right at home on display in an art gallery (even one in a school gym), and usually I'd be much more proud and thrilled to see him and my other characters, but right now I've got to focus.

"Hey, I have some punch. Want some?" I ask them both.

They look at each other. Dad asks if Terri wants it. She says, "No, not right now." So I hold it out to Dad. He shrugs and takes it.

I stare at him—probably a little like a weirdo—as he lifts the cup toward his lips.

Then he stops and nods toward my storyboard. "Cleo, how long did you work on this?" he asks. "You never even showed it to me."

"A long time. I don't know. We can talk about it later," I say impatiently, staring at the drink so passionately that if my eyes were lasers, they'd drill holes in the cup and the punch would spill all over him. *Drink, Dad! Drink, drink, drink!*

"It's so fun and action-packed. I like it." He raises his cup again. His mouth opens slightly . . . to speak more words. "Your classmates really worked hard too."

"Yeah, yeah, I'm sure they all did." *Who cares, Dad? Aren't you thirsty? Why are you boring Terri with all this talk of my artwork when the two of you could already be falling back in love?*

"I really think you could have a career in this." Dad gestures at my storyboard with the cup of punch. Why isn't he drinking it?

"I'm really proud of you," he says . . . and finally, *finally* takes a sip. Yes!

He has an uncertain expression for a second but doesn't mention anything about the taste.

I know time doesn't really stand still, but it might as well. I'm not hearing the music anymore. I'm not worried about Lisa Lee and the spots on her suede. I'm not thinking about whether or not things are working out with Madison and Sam and Larry—well, not really. All I'm doing is shouting (inside my head, of course), *Say something, Dad! Say something to Terri right now!* But he's taking another long, leisurely sip of his punch. *Come on, Dad! A minute ago you were avoiding the punch with every comment you could think of. Now you love it?*

Ten little words, Dad! Talk to Terri about anything! Life on Mars, the mess I made in the kitchen, whether or not her cat sheds in the summer. I don't care; just say something to her!

Finally Dad speaks. "Hey! I'm surprised we didn't see you already tonight. How are you doing?" In my head, I count the number of words Dad just said. It's more than ten. The only problem is that Dad was not looking at Terri when he said them. I turn my head in the direction he's facing.

It's Paige.

Samantha's mom. A third wheel on what should have been a bicycle. Looking perfect as always with her long, shiny black hair and tight-fitting skirt and blouse.

"Good to see you, Bradley," Paige says, leaning in to kiss the air beside his cheek. Oh no! Sam's mom liked him once, and now if the love potion works, he's not only going to like her back, he's going to *love* her!

And it will be all my fault.

9

The adults are all friendly and smiley as Dad introduces Terri to Paige. Dad's plenty chatty, sharing lots and lots of words with Terri now that it's too late.

When Terri broke up with Dad, I remember her being upset—well, not really upset, but sad—thinking Dad was spending a lot of time with Paige. That was back when Samantha and I were so close we wanted to be sisters, and we thought if her mom married my dad, it would be the best thing ever. But I know better now. If I know anything about love—and I'm definitely learning a lot from Ryder Landry's songs—there's a person out there who's right for you. Ryder calls it your *Only One.* Sure, people can date and like each other and even think they're in love, but there's only one *real* one out there. One *right* one.

Terri is definitely Dad's *Only One.*

When there's a pause in the conversation, Dad takes another sip of his drink and makes a face. "That is really . . . unusual punch," he says.

Really, Dad? I think. *If you thought it was that interesting, why didn't you tell Terri when you needed to?*

I stand there, stunned by everything that's happened. There's only one thing I can do now, and it's the opposite of what I thought I'd want tonight.

I have to hope the love potion doesn't work.

Standing with Dad, Terri, and Paige, I want to get away as fast as possible. "I've . . . uh . . . gotta go," I say. "I still haven't seen Madison's or Sam's stuff. Bye!"

I zoom through our art gallery gym, frantically searching for Madison . . . Sam . . . Larry . . . Ryder Landry's head . . . anything to get away from the big, dumb mistake I made. I need to warn Madison *not* to do anything. I should have known better than to mess with magic. Something can always go wrong. I just forgot for one tiny moment. But I can't give up now, because I need to fix what I've done. And how in the world am I supposed to do that?

Down an aisle my eye catches a glimpse of yellow hair, puffier and even more canary-colored than Mrs. Paddington's.

It's Ryder Landry's head—with a wig on top, it looks like.

In front of the head is Madison. Alone. Maybe that's good. Maybe nothing else has gone wrong.

I join her. "Ryder looks great," I say. I have to say something.

"Oh, he looks bad," she says. "I couldn't make the hair work with chicken wire, so my mom gave me a wig, but I'm about as good a hairdresser as I am at papier-mâché."

Before I knew Madison for real, I thought she was great at everything. Now I look at Ryder—skin too orange, teeth too big and white, eyelashes too fake—and I know Madison isn't perfect. I like that in a friend, I decide. Samantha isn't perfect either. I wish we could all be imperfect together.

"No, he's totally cute," I say, just to be nice.

Madison looks at me seriously. "Something went wrong," she says.

Oh no! Madison's a bad artist *and* she makes mistakes just like I do? She's even more imperfect than I thought!

I want to know every detail, so I have to tell her the truth. "Something went wrong with me too."

"What happened?" she asks. I look into Ryder Landry's unnaturally blue eyes and tell her the whole story.

"We'll fix it," Madison promises. "We're smart. We've got the book. There'll be a way to undo it, for sure."

I like hearing all this, though there's no way of knowing if any of it is true. But now I need to find out what *else* happened.

"What went wrong for you?" I finally ask. "Did Larry drink the potion?"

Madison is about to answer when a voice interrupts us.

"Hey, Cleo, I haven't seen your project yet. Where is it?" I turn to see Larry sipping from a blue cup, his headphones sitting around his neck.

Madison and I aren't thrilled with the interruption, but it's not his fault. He doesn't know. "Over with the drawings and paintings," I tell him. I notice that his music is still filling the gym. "Hey, how is your music still playing if you're here with us?"

"I made a playlist long enough to let me take a break. I had to see what my compadres were up to and toast to their success!" He lifts his cup in the air, then drinks. "Aaaack!" he screams, pointing at Madison's Ryder Landry head. "What's that?"

"Oh, leave me alone!" Madison tells him. "That's Ryder Landry and you know it."

"Ryder Landry again?" Larry makes a barfing motion. "Don't you ladies know there are awesome dudes like me right here at school?" He throws his arm over my shoulder and starts singing at the top of his lungs. *"You, you, you plus me, me, me. Put us together, it's chemistry!"*

I wriggle out from underneath, laughing. "You know his songs way too well to blame it on your little sister!"

Madison points in the direction of the DJ table. "Go play that song right now!"

"I'll get right on that . . . after I've played every other song known to man!" Larry says, strolling away. Then he

turns and winks at both of us. "Have a good night, ladies."
Bowing toward me, he adds, "Cleo," like one of King
Arthur's knights.

"I like him, but he can really be annoying sometimes," I
say to Madison. "Now, what happened?" I pause and make
sure Larry is far enough away so he won't hear me. "So . . .
did he drink the potion or not?"

"No," Madison says, disappointed.

"Well, maybe that's a good thing—"

Madison cuts me off. "It's not good. I was mixing up the
potion in some lemonade and Sam came back."

She's right. That's not good. "Did she see you do it?"

"No, not really, but she was all suspicious like before."

"You didn't . . . *give* it to her, did you?" I ask. If Samantha drank the potion without Larry around, she could've
talked to . . . anyone after that. A teacher, a cafeteria worker,
the hamster in the fourth-grade classroom. Anyone!

"No, no, no. But she was asking and asking. She really
wasn't letting it go."

I smile. Samantha's like Toby when he wants to be taken
on a walk or play with his favorite squeaky toy. When she
puts her mind to something, she usually gets it.

"I had to get her to stop, so I told her to go find you and
check out your drawings."

"Well, that's okay," I say with a sigh. But I can tell there's
more to come.

Madison takes a deep breath. She looks at her Ryder

Landry head as if he'll help her say the next thing. "I put it down."

"Put what down?" I ask.

"The lemonade. When I was talking to Sam."

"What do you mean?" I'm afraid I already know what she means, but I want to be sure.

"I left the lemonade on the table."

"O . . . kay," I reply, thinking it over. "That's not so bad, though. You wouldn't drink a lemonade you didn't pour, right?"

"I was hoping that, but when Sam walked away, I turned around and it was gone."

"The lemonade . . . with the potion in it . . . was gone?"

Madison nods, biting her lip and picking at her nail cuticles. She looks worried, frustrated, and almost scared. So I try to make her feel better.

"I'm sure someone threw it out."

"You think so?" Madison's blue eyes look hopeful.

"Sure," I say. But inside I'm imagining everything that could have gone wrong: A teacher drank it and then talked to a student. . . . A student drank it and then talked to a teacher. . . . Lisa Lee drank it and then talked to the papier-mâché Ryder Landry head. . . .

This is a problem. More than a problem. This could be big, big trouble—at school and at home. Madison must think everything's okay, though, because she's already smiling again, ready to check out more artwork. I smile too, but I feel like my heart has turned into a block of cement.

What in the world happened to that cup of lemonade?

Dad seems happier than usual over the weekend . . . and I don't like it.

I wake up Saturday morning to Toby yowling at the foot of my bed like one of the coyotes we sometimes hear in our neighborhood. But his howls are only the second-most annoying sound I hear. Far away in the kitchen, a loud, mechanical grinding sound keeps going on and on—GRRRRRRR! GRRRRRRR!—starting, stopping, then starting again. From my bed, I call Toby over and pat him on the head to calm him down. Then I get up with a groan and shuffle down the hall. "Dad? What's that noise?"

Inside the kitchen there's an unusual sight. Dad is dressed—in clothes, not the underwear and T-shirt he usually wears until at least noon on the weekend. His hair almost looks brushed, and he's even wearing laced-up sneakers instead of flip-flops.

He pushes a button on the blender, and the noise grinds to a halt. "Remember that one week when we tried to eat more green foods? After your healthy play?"

Of course I do. Yuck.

"I know that didn't work out for us," he admits, "so I'm

trying something better—homemade smoothies!" Dad is so excited you'd think he whipped up a pot of gold coins and cupcakes. "I know you like strawberries and blueberries and bananas, but I mixed in the *really* healthy stuff so sneakily you won't even be able to taste it."

I pull out a chair and sit at the table. "Why are you in such a good mood?" I ask.

"Oh, I don't know," Dad says. "It was nice seeing your artwork last night and talking to your friends."

And seeing Terri? I wonder. No, more likely he's happy he saw Paige. Ugh. Maybe I once thought she was cool and pretty and had lots to teach me, but now I don't want her anywhere around Dad. I want Samantha to be my friend, not my sister. And I want Dad to be with his *Only One.*

Dad pours the thick purple smoothie into two big cups. He hands me one with a yellow smiley face on it. The smile matches his.

"Thanks," I say with no enthusiasm whatsoever. "I'm going back to my room."

"Okay, but don't stay there all day. It's too nice a day to waste!"

"Cool, Dad." I'm walking away so he doesn't see my frown.

When Dad and Terri broke up, Dad sat at his computer day and night with his shoulders slumped. Our curtains were closed, keeping out the sunlight. Mounds of dust and Toby hair started piling up in corners. I didn't like any of that. But Dad being in a good mood isn't much better. It's irritating, especially when all I want to do is look through *POCIÓNES FANTÁSTICOS* and figure out if there's any way to turn a love potion around so he and Paige *don't* fall in love. I have no free time the entire weekend, though, because Dad bursts into my room wanting to go to an art museum downtown. Later we pull weeds in the backyard, and on Sunday we go for a bike ride around the lake! We pass Red Shorts twice. First he's just walking fast, but the next time he's reading a magazine too. Dad says hello, and Red Shorts nods back as usual.

Finally, on Sunday night, I text Madison and tell her I haven't gotten even one baby step closer to finding a potion that could reverse the charm we put on Dad. And by the time Monday morning rolls around, I'm exhausted—and actually happy to be going back to school.

I'm happy, that is, until I get there. As soon as Dad parks by the curb in the parking lot, I'm ready to run for Kevin's classroom. Then Sam and her mom pull up right behind us.

Dad looks in the rearview mirror. "Is that Samantha?"

Of course it is, but I don't want Dad seeing Paige, so I say, "I don't think so," and open my door to jump out. "You'd better go, Dad. I'm sure you have a lot of work to do!" I take a few steps toward the school, but his car doesn't pull away.

Instead, the driver's side door opens. Dad is getting out! I watch helplessly as he walks over to Sam's car and starts talking to Paige through her open window. I can't hear what they're saying, but it doesn't matter. Why are they talking at all? How often has this been happening? Is this the first time they've talked since the art show?

Suddenly Sam is standing next to me. As if she heard my thoughts, she says, "I think my mom and your dad talked over the weekend."

I stare into the parking lot at Dad leaning over Paige's car. It's easy to imagine what they're saying: *"You're so hand-some, Bradley." "You look so pretty today, Paige." "I like you." "I like you more." "Let's kiss." "Not here, where the kids can see." "Later, then." "Okay." "You're so cute." "I really like you." "Not as much as I like you."*

Argh! How can this be happening? The love potion recipe said it was foolproof, and it was. I'm the fool, and I proved it worked—the wrong way, with the wrong people.

I turn to Samantha to start up a conversation—a conversation that friends might have, *not* sisters—but she's already gone. She's a dot across the courtyard, heading toward Kevin's classroom.

10

It's a happy announcement when we hear that instead of Recreational Wellness this afternoon, there's going to be an assembly. I love school assemblies; they're great for napping. No matter what the topic is—William Shakespeare's birthday, not talking to strangers, how to prepare for an earthquake—it's almost impossible not to snooze. If the lights are down and the speaker has a calm, mellow voice, my eyes droop and close immediately. Once, in fourth grade, I guess I even snored, because my friend Jane Anne had to jab me with her elbow so I'd wake up. I wonder if that's why she didn't want to be my friend the next year.

I hope Madison doesn't mind a little snoring, because I'm settling into a chair in the auditorium, getting comfy. She's beside me, but she's sitting up straight, all alert and excited. A second later, I realize why.

This is no ordinary assembly.

"Summertime, summertime, sum-sum-summertime!" An old-timey song blasts through the room. Brightly colored lights flash on and off, and all the kids begin hollering and cheering. The song changes to a slow one: *"Because it's summer, summertime is here . . ."*

Madison leans over to me and whispers, though she really should yell because the music changes to the type of old rock song my dad might like: *"Hot time, summer in the city . . ."*

"This is the summer assembly," Madison says.

Duh, I think, but I say, "Yeah, I got that idea. What's so big about it?"

Before she can answer me, our principal, Frederick, walks onto the stage. He usually wears a tie, or at least a professional-looking sweater, but today he's in board shorts and a Hawaiian shirt! He's also wearing flip-flops and sunglasses and has a triangle of white on his nose like he's afraid of sunburn. "Only two weeks of school left!" he shouts into a microphone. "So it's time to begin the countdown!"

"Countdown to what?" I ask Madison. She starts to answer, but Frederick's voice booms through the auditorium.

"The countdown to . . ."

"THE BLING BLING SUMMER FLING!" yells everyone in the audience but me. I look around in shock. Sometimes I forget it's still my first year at Friendship Community School, but this definitely reminds me.

"What is—" I start to ask Madison, but she points toward the front and says, "You'll see."

I see, all right. Suddenly girls from the gymnastics squad are doing cartwheels and handsprings across the stage. Boys from the football team walk on with cheerleaders on their shoulders, and when the girls jump off and turn around, I can see the words *BLING BLING* spelled out in big letters on the back of each uniform. All around me kids are hooting and shouting; some are standing and dancing to the music. A few rows down I see even Samantha clapping, and she never lets anything school-related thrill her!

I stop asking questions and watch the spectacle. Then something makes me want to turn away. Lisa Lee and Kylie Mae enter the stage from opposite sides, sort of singing, sort of rapping.

> *"There's a time of year that rocks for all*
> *It's not spring or winter and never fall*
> *The time you love, unless you're a fool*
> *Is the time we take a break from school."*

Then Lisa Lee yells, "Summer!" and Kylie Mae replies, "Fling!" and they repeat it again and again. Everyone around me shouts along. It'd be easy enough to join in, but I'm dying to know what this Bling Bling Summer Fling thing *is*! I turn toward Madison for an answer—but she's not there.

I look at the row across the aisle. I look behind me. Did she need to go to the bathroom? It's weird she wouldn't have said so. Finally I turn toward the front of the auditorium—and that's where I find her.

Onstage. With Lisa Lee and Kylie Mae, looking like they belong together. All three of them do the next section of the rap, with coordinated dance and hand movements.

Pointing at themselves, they shout, "When we say 'summer,' you say . . ."

"FLING!" shouts the audience.

"When we say 'bling bling,' you say . . ."

"FLING!"

The shouting goes back and forth until the background music ends. Madison, Lisa Lee, and Kylie Mae all smile and wave, and as they skip offstage, Lisa Lee and Kylie Mae put their arms around Madison, and they look like the happiest three friends in the world. Just like they once were.

And by the looks of what just happened, they might be again.

Frederick comes back out in his beach clothes, and though I'm probably the only kid who needs to know, he explains what the heck is going on. "Yes, students, in two short weeks it'll be time for the Bling Bling Summer Fling, and this year we have planned the best one ever!"

I want to pay attention and learn more, but every few seconds I turn to the empty seat next to mine. Where is Madison?

"This year," Frederick announces, "the Bling Bling is going to be at Hollywoodland Park."

I've heard some big cheers today, but the one that follows is the biggest yet. Kids are high-fiving, jumping out of their chairs, and screaming as if a talk show host just gave them a new car or a trip to Australia. I'm a little excited myself. I've heard of Hollywoodland Park. It has the tallest roller coasters, the slipperiest waterslides, and the fastest-spinning rides anywhere. And because it's Hollywoodland, famous movie monsters and superheroes wander the park, and the bumper cars are Ferraris and Maseratis.

A night there would definitely be cool. Especially with a friend like Madison.

But why isn't she back in her seat next to me?

When the assembly ends, everyone leaves the auditorium talking enthusiastically with friends and making plans for the big event. The auditorium is almost completely empty when someone shouts my name. But it's not Madison. It's Larry, with his backpack over his shoulder. "Come on, Cleo, it's outdoor break. Meet me at the jungle gym!"

Though I'd like to wait longer, I force myself to get up. I look around once more, then slowly make my way outside. Larry's sitting on the pavement alone except for Mono, his little carved monkey. I still don't see Madison anywhere.

"So. Now you know about the Bling Bling Summer Fling," Larry says.

"Not really," I say, sitting down. "I get that it's a trip to an amusement park. But what's the big deal?"

"Oh, it's not really a big deal," he says all casual, then raises his voice louder and louder with every word that follows. "Unless you think that the *most awesome night in the history of the universe* is not a big deal!"

Larry's trademark sarcasm.

"So it's *not* a big deal?" I ask.

"No, it's always cool. It's just a little cooler for the popular kids."

Popular kids. Lisa Lee. Kylie Mae. Their boyfriends. Madison.

"It's been happening at Friendship Community forever, I guess," Larry tells me. "Each year we do something different. Like the zoo. Or a carnival. Or a big party at a rich person's house. It's the last time to have a blast with your best friends before we all go our separate ways for the summer."

"Where's everybody going?" As far as I know, I'm not going anywhere. My idea of summer vacation would be Madison's awesome pool and backyard.

"Well, everybody goes somewhere different. Like, I'm going to computer camp, then science camp, and then my family will probably go to Europe or something."

"So you're not home at all, all summer?"

"No. Hardly anybody is."

"What does Madison do?"

"Oh, she doesn't go to any dorky camps like I do. I think she always goes to Hawaii."

"All summer?" I ask. Why hasn't Madison ever mentioned this before?

"I think so. Her parents have a big, huge house there, and they share it with Lisa Lee's family. Kylie Mae goes too. At least I'm pretty sure they all went last summer, because at the beginning of the school year they were all real tan and wore matching flowery dresses on the first day."

Lisa Lee, Kylie Mae, and Madison—spending the whole summer together? No wonder this Bling Bling Summer Fling is so important! It's your last chance to hang out with your friends . . . unless those friends are going to *Hawaii* with you! And if Madison spends three months back with her old friends—the friends she just *rapped* with onstage!—I may never get her back.

"Hey, did you see me in the big show?"

I look up and Madison is walking toward us. She remembers us, thank goodness.

"Yeah, you were great," says Larry. "Like old times."

Madison climbs onto the jungle gym and hangs upside down. "I couldn't resist. How many years have I done that song with them?"

"Ever since I can remember," Larry tells her.

"YOU WERE REALLY GOOD!" I say—way too loud, way too excited. "THE SUMMER FLING SOUNDS

REALLY COOL!" *Calm down, Cleo, I tell myself. Don't scare Madison away before she even leaves for Hawaii!*

"We usually call it the Bling Bling," she tells me. "But, oh, right, you wouldn't know. It's your first one. You're gonna love it."

I sure hope so.

Lisa Lee and Kylie Mae stroll across the courtyard with Ronnie and Lonnie. "That was awesome, Madison!" Lisa Lee shouts. "You'll have to come to the Bling Bling with us, and we'll have the funnest time ever!"

Madison smiles and waves. She looks happy.

Too happy.

As they walk away, Larry jumps up. "What are they talking about?" he says to us. "*We're* the funnest people in the world!"

"Don't you mean 'most fun,' smarty-pants?" Madison asks.

"No, I mean we're refugees from the planet Fun, and we're called Funnes. So we're the Funnes people in the world. We're actually the only Funnes people on Earth."

Madison and I started hearing Larry's bizarre stories when we were in the *Healthyland* play together. At first he seemed like what my dad would call a "goofball," but now we love when he talks like this.

"So are we from outer space, or are we regular people?" I ask.

"Well, to Earthlings we're from outer space, but we're

regular people on planet Fun." Larry's hands plunge into his backpack and he pulls out a tube made of paper with a pointy cone at the top, wrapped around a little plastic canister poking out the bottom. "Actually, we got here in this rocket ship!"

I look at Madison and we both shake our heads. Then we just lean back on the grass to enjoy the show.

Larry stands in front of us like he's doing stand-up comedy or a magic show. "Before we left planet Fun, we had to fill our rocket ship with fuel." He pulls a bottle of water out of his backpack and pours it into the canister at the bottom of his "rocket."

"Here on Earth, they call it water. These silly people drink it. Some of them even bathe in it."

"Though you're not one of them," I joke. He and Madison laugh.

"No, I am not. I would not bathe in the precious fuel of planet Fun. On our planet, water powers everything. If only these stupid Earth humans would learn how to run cars and planes on water like we do."

"Yes, we're brilliant," Madison says.

"Hey, we were brilliant enough to get to Earth," Larry says, dropping a little white tablet—it looks a lot like the mint Kevin dropped into the soda bottle—into the canister. He puts the top on and puts the rocket on the ground so it's facing toward the sky.

"Watch out!" he warns us and steps back. And sure

enough, a second later there's a small POP! sound and his rocket flies into the air, fizzy water spraying from the bottom of it. It doesn't shoot up far enough to get us to another planet—it's not even far enough to get to the top of the jungle gym—but it's still a pretty good trick.

Madison and I cheer. "I think that was . . . chemistry!" I say.

"*It's a reaction, an attraction!*" Madison sings, jumping up to dance.

I join in. "*Put us together and there's plenty of action!*"

Lisa Lee and Kylie Mae look at us across the schoolyard with their usual sourpuss faces, but then they smile. The next thing I know, they're laughing and pointing at Larry. Then they shout for Ronnie and Lonnie to come over and look too.

I notice what they're seeing at the same time Larry does. Some of the water splattered on him and it looks like he peed his pants. We all know he didn't, but that's probably not the story Lisa Lee and Kylie Mae will tell their friends.

Larry's face turns red as he puts one hand over the front of his pants and runs toward his backpack and his carved monkey. He scoops them up with his other hand and scurries toward the school. "Gotta run, see ya later!" he shouts as he goes. "Cleo, will you pick up the rest of my stuff?"

Madison looks at me and sighs. "Sometimes Larry makes it really hard to stand up for him." Then she shouts across the courtyard to Lisa Lee and Kylie Mae. "Be nice!"

They roll their eyes and nod. After that they walk toward the basketball court holding hands with Ronnie and Lonnie, so hopefully Larry won't have to suffer anything else from them.

I stand up to gather the pieces of Larry's rocket. I pick up the canister and its top, then the tube made of light cardboard. It had Scotch tape holding it closed, but the force of the launch—or the crash back to Earth—tore it open. Inside, there's writing on the paper.

What I read is the last thing in the world I expected. Specific directions to planet Fun would have been less surprising.

"What is it?" Madison asks.

I show her.

It's a note. Written in red crayon, in messy cursive writing, is one question with two answers.

Do you like me? Yes or no. Check one.

There are boxes next to YES and NO.

Madison reads it, then looks at me, her eyes wide with shock.

"That's for *you*," she says. "Larry told you to pick it up."

We look at each other. Neither of us knows what to say.

"No," I sputter, shaking my head in disbelief. "That's crazy pants."

"Crazy pants pulled way up high with a belt."

"Larry . . . likes . . . me?" It's so crazy pants, I can barely get the words out.

"He *likes* you likes you. *Boyfriend-girlfriend* likes you."

"But I don't want him to boyfriend-girlfriend like me. I'm only eleven!"

Madison looks at me seriously. "I don't think you have a choice."

"Ewww!" As soon as I make the noise, I feel bad. It's the kind of "ewww" Lisa Lee or Kylie Mae would say when they look at Larry . . . or me. "I mean, I *like* Larry," I try to explain to Madison, "but I don't . . ."

I don't have to finish the sentence. Madison understands.

"Maybe it's a joke," I say. I don't really think it is, but right now I'm looking for any other explanation.

"You think it's a joke?" Madison asks.

"It's gotta be, right?"

"I don't know."

I have to say the truth. "Doesn't seem like a joke."

Madison agrees. She looks at the note again. DO YOU LIKE ME? YES OR NO. CHECK ONE. "I know. Seems real."

"Really real."

"Really real but really strange."

We sit in silence for a few seconds. This is way wrong. Larry is supposed to like Samantha—not me—so we can all be one big happy family of friends. Larry liking *me* ruins everything.

The bell rings that it's time to go back to class, and as we jump to our feet, it hits me. "Oh my gosh, Madison! This is *love potion* real."

Madison looks at me in shock. We head toward the school, talking as fast as we're walking. "Larry drank the lemonade?" she asks.

"There's no other explanation. I must have been the first person he talked to after he drank it!"

"What do we do, then?"

"We've got to reverse it."

Just saying the words fills me with fear. It was going to be hard enough to get my dad to change his mind about Paige; now we have to make Larry fall out of love with me too—definitely before Sam finds out. Because if Sam likes him as much as she liked my voodoo doll, she could do some pretty extreme things. I've seen it before.

I can't let that happen. Not this time.

When Dad picks me up at school, he has no idea how my life has changed. It's the first time someone has been in love with his daughter . . . but judging by our normal, boring conversation, he sees no difference in me.

When we get out of the car at home, he says, like it's nothing important at all, "Oh, something came for you today. I put it by your millipede terrarium."

Now, this is news! I run toward my room without taking off my backpack, without kicking off my sneakers, without saying "thanks" to Dad or anything. Finally, Uncle Arnie must have sent the instructions for the love potion, right when I need them most! Uncle Arnie is a genius! Uncle Arnie is a wizard! Uncle Arnie is the best!

I throw open my door.

Uncle Arnie sent another postcard. Disappointment!

This one is from Barney Smith's Toilet Seat Art Museum

in San Antonio. The picture shows a smiling man, like a hundred years old, standing in a garage filled with toilet seats from floor to ceiling. All of them have paintings—or even sculptures—on them. I see American flags, Michael Jackson, and even—if I'm reading it right—a tribute to modern dentistry, with dental instruments and fake teeth on it! This guy and Uncle Arnie seem like the type who would be friends for sure.

I turn over the postcard. On the back it says:

A journey of two thousand miles begins with a single step. I'm taking that step! How about you? No one can do it but why-owe-ewe, Cleo!

Hmmm. This one is tougher to figure out than his first one.

For one thing, I don't think his message on the back has anything to do with Barney Smith's Toilet Seat Art Museum. And it definitely doesn't seem very specific about the love potion he sent. But it must mean something.

I think it over for a while, but nothing goes through my brain. Just air. Wind. Tumbleweeds.

Roberta has said in Focus! class that if you're stuck, sometimes you should do something else with your mind; then an answer might come. So I open *Quantum Physics, Biocentrism, and the Universe as We Know It* and read a few sentences.

In the mathematically rigorous formulation of quantum mechanics, the possible states of a quantum mechanical system are represented by unit vectors. Each observable is represented by a maximally linear operator acting on the state space.

I read the sentences over and over again, but they are of no help at all. Do people really talk like this? Do scientists really understand this stuff? I need to remember to talk to Kevin and get a new book, because right now I've got a one-word book report that goes like this: *Huh?*

Roberta's trick is not working—reading this ridiculous stuff is only frustrating me more. Plus, my mind keeps wandering back to the postcard. Why "a journey of two thousand miles"? And what is "why-owe-ewe"? A ewe is a female sheep, right? Why would Uncle Arnie owe a female sheep anything?

When Dad calls me for dinner—his special burgers from the grill, with cheese and bacon bits inside—I show him the postcard. "Don't get grease on it," I warn him.

He gives me a funny look as he wipes his hands on a paper towel. "Boy, you are very protective of your postcards." He looks at the photo and laughs, then reads the back. "I think it's 'a journey of a *thousand* miles,'" he says, handing it back to me. "But I guess it's nice that your uncle is sending you inspirational cards, whether he gets the quotes right or not."

"And what does he owe a ewe?" I ask.

Dad looks confused.

I take the postcard back and read the line. "No one can do it but why-owe-ewe."

"Say it out loud again," Dad tells me. "You'll figure it out."

I whisper it a few times as I take my last bite of burger and put my plate in the sink. "Got it yet?" Dad asks.

Finally I get it. "Ohhh! Y-O-U! *You!*"

"Uncle Arnie's clever that way," Dad says. "Now go do your homework. I'll do the dishes. Come back later and put them away."

I walk to my room, wishing Uncle Arnie weren't so clever. I wish he'd just tell me what to do.

Or *is* he telling me what to do?

I read the postcard again.

I'm taking that step! . . . No one can do it but you.

Uncle Arnie must be saying that I can't sit around and wait. Like the first postcard—I need to take charge. And he's right. Now that Larry has announced his love for me (pretty much!), and Dad is talking to Paige (way too much!), I need to do something. Tonight. I need to take that step.

I wriggle under my bed and grab *POCIÓNES FAN-TÁSTICOS*. I flip through the pages. *Corazón. Vida. Cariño.* So much Spanish!

I look at the illustrations with my best, most focused attention to see if any of them suggest the idea of reversing a potion. Page after page shows hearts and flowers and pretty things. People looking lovingly into each other's eyes. A couple running through a meadow holding hands in the sunshine.

Ugh. Why does there have to be so much *love* in a love potion book? Why does everybody need to be in love? What's wrong with being friends? It seems a lot simpler to me! Why wasn't Larry happy with friendship? Now everything is going to be uncomfortable and weird and awkward. Just his note was bad enough. It made me feel all nervous and hot and jumpy. I'm not going to know what to say or how to act around him, and I don't want to hurt his feelings, but I don't want him to think I like him that way because I don't. Samantha does! And if I want her to be my friend, she can't think I like Larry back.

Help me, *POCIÓNES FANTÁSTICOS!*

Finally, I come across a drawing that makes me stop. It couldn't be more obvious: there's an upside-down heart with a red circle around it and a line through it. *No love!* Yes! That's exactly what I want!

There are other drawings on the page too. Thin green leaves go up and down the side. There's also a pillow on a bed . . . and a bathtub. I wonder what all that's for.

I don't want to make Dad suspicious by using his scanner to copy the recipe while he's in the kitchen, so I type the Spanish words into my computer. When it's finished, I put the text into the translation program, and it comes out like this, I think:

This potion is not to drink; this potion will sur-
round your entire body and person! Firstly, you
must take fifty to one hundred bay leaves and
pour them into a bath hot on a night dark.

Oh, right. The adjective-noun *problema.*

Relax in your bath hot for a ten minutes luxurious.
Think of the person unfortunate you do not or no
longer love with your heart full. Calmly emerge
from the bath and put on nightclothes washed
freshly. Pin a bay leaf extra to each corner of
your pillow and place a fifth leaf underneath it.
Climb into a bed cozy and you will dream of the
person sad you love no longer. The time next you
see this person, the love for you will be gone.

This sounds great—not just for me and Larry, but for
Dad and Paige too—but there's one problem. I've never
heard of bay leaves. Thank goodness for the computer. Back
in the olden days, according to Dad, if you didn't know a
fact, you had to look it up in an encyclopedia—and if you
didn't have one at home, you had to go to a library. This
makes me happy I'm alive now and not then!

Online I learn that bay leaves are used in cooking to
add flavor to stews, soups, and pâtés (whatever those are),
and you can buy the leaves in a jar at the store. Dad's never

made a stew, but he's got a lot of weird spices, with names like cumin and marjoram, so he may have bay leaves too.

Dad's on the couch reading when I walk toward the kitchen. It must be a really good book because he says, "Hey, Cleo," without even looking up at me. Perfect.

Outside the kitchen window, the sun is starting to set. It's not a "night dark" yet, but hopefully it will be by the time I finish. I rummage through the cabinet with our spices, and sure enough, there's a dusty jar of bay leaves Dad has probably never used. I look inside. Unlike most of our spices, which are pulverized into little sandy granules, bay leaves actually look like little leaves from a tree.

I take a sniff, then pull my nose back quickly. They don't smell bad, but they're sharp and spicy, with a little whiff of the bottom of a wooden drawer mixed in. Whoever thought to put these in *food*?

Hiding the jar in the palm of my hand, I walk past Dad and into the bathroom, then turn on the hot water. As I wait for the tub to fill, I pull out five leaves to save for my pillow. They feel brittle, like old-fashioned paper that rips easily, so I'm super careful as I place them on the edge of the sink. Then I pour the whole jar into the bath. I hope there are at least fifty in there! The leaves spread out fast, like water bugs swimming on the surface.

When the tub is past the halfway mark and the bathroom is filled with steam that smells like spice and dirt, I turn off the faucet, throw all my clothes on the floor, and dip my foot in. Yow! It's way too hot.

I turn on a trickle of cold water to cool it down, then wrap a towel around me and walk across the hall to my bedroom. Playing with my millipede will be more interesting than sitting and waiting for a bath to get to the right temperature. But as I put my hand in Millie's terrarium, something else in my room catches my eye.

It's the love potion, of course—right on my dresser like always, the small red bottle sparkling under my overhead light.

I can't help thinking that Uncle Arnie's love potion would definitely make my bay leaf bath work even better. It's sitting there, waiting to be used. Wanting to be used. And I wouldn't even use the whole bottle, I tell myself. Just one big, fat drop plopped into a bathtub full of bay leaves might do the trick. And even if it *doesn't* help, how much could it hurt?

The problem is, I don't know the answers to those questions, and I can't stand it anymore. It's been over a month since I got the potion, and I've been patient enough! I need to find out how it works.

I'm doing it. I'm calling Uncle Arnie.

I sit at my desk and click on his name. I hope it's not too late to call New Orleans, but Uncle Arnie doesn't seem like the type to go to sleep early. After a bunch of rings, though,

I'm ready to give up. He's probably in his own bath playing with rubber duckies or out concocting more ways to confuse me. I guess it just wasn't meant to be.

My finger is about to press "end" when a screen suddenly clicks on. No one says hello, though. The screen is a filmy white, like a sheet or something is hanging over the computer. Behind it I can see Uncle Arnie's living room, the mess it always is. I start to say a quiet, uncertain "hello" when a loud female voice bursts through my speakers.

"What in the world was that?" it asks. It sounds like an older lady, with a Southern accent so strong it almost sounds fake.

"I think it's his phone, Mama," says another Southern voice, a younger lady.

"His computer is a phone? How can he lift it up to his ear?" the older lady crows. Then, without warning, her face fills Uncle Arnie's screen. All I see is long, fuzzy, mostly gray hair and bushy, dark eyebrows—kind of like a female Uncle Arnie. But I only see her for a second because I leap out of my chair and squat on the floor, out of view.

"I saw someone, there on that screen!" she screams. "A little girl with yellow hair."

Poop! She saw me!

"Well, she's not there now," the younger voice says.

"What's that, then?" says the old lady. "As sure as the day is long and the grass is growin', that looks like the top of a blond head."

Poop, poop, poop! I throw myself flat on the floor so I can't be seen at all.

"I don't see anything, Mama."

The older voice gets closer to the computer's microphone. "Well, now it's gone! I don't know if it was a ghost or a demon disguised as an angel, but it was there!" I hear a banging sound, like she's hitting the computer. "Come back, ghost child! Tell us what life is like in the beyond."

I stay flat on the floor, staring at my ceiling. Who *are* these people?

"We'd better turn it off, Mama," says the younger voice. And a moment later, I don't hear any sounds at all.

I stay on the floor, too scared to move. I want to make sure those people are truly gone and Uncle Arnie's computer is really off before I get up.

I lift my head slowly. "Hello?" I say quietly.

There's no response, so I sit up halfway.

"I am the ghost child of Los Angeles!" I whisper in a spooky voice. When I don't hear any answer to that, I feel safer. I glance at the computer screen. It's black on Uncle Arnie's side.

My heart is going wild and a million questions are running through my head. Then I remember something else that's running—the bathtub! I dart across the hall, where the water has inched up and up and is about to go over the edge! I turn off the faucet just in time.

That was a close one. There'd be no way to explain to

Dad an overflowing tub or the smell in the bathroom right now. I need to forget about whatever weirdness is going on at Uncle Arnie's and start working on my own weirdness, without his love potion. I'm too freaked out from what just happened to even think about using it now!

After letting some water drain out, I get into the tub slowly, like a corn dog being dipped in its bubbling batter. Once I'm all the way in, I lift my toes out of the water and see them getting red—with the rest of my body quickly following. To get my mind off that, I pretend like I'm Madison's mom, Heather Paddington, in her gigantic "powder room," filled with big bottles of perfume and vases of flowers. I lie back, put a washcloth over my eyes, and order my staff around. "Chef, make me some pâté, and use extra bay leaves!" "Alfredo, more bubbles! But *close your eyes* when you come in!"

KNOCK KNOCK. What's that? Why is there knocking? The chef isn't really here! And I'm not even sure Alfredo is a real person! I sit up and pull the cloth off my eyes. "What?" I shout.

Dad's voice comes from the other side of the door. "Who are you talking to?"

"Nobody," I say. "I'm just taking a bath."

"You don't have your phone in there, do you?"

I know why Dad's asking. If I were talking on the phone in the tub, I would drop it for sure. "No. I was . . . um . . . talking to myself, I guess."

"Well, as long as you're good company," he says. What a doofus. "Don't forget to come out and put the dishes away tonight."

I tell him I won't . . . forget, that is. Then I dunk myself under the water. If I'm going to be covered in a bay leaf broth, it might as well be from head to toe.

12

After I drain the tub, I wrap a towel around me and run to my room, holding my five leftover bay leaves like they're precious diamonds. Toby, who's lying on the floor, looks up and makes a grossed-out face. "Oh, like you always smell like roses!" I say as I open my dresser drawer. None of my pj's—or, as the potion called them, nightclothes— are "washed freshly," but I pick a nightgown I haven't worn since I was nine, so I'm pretty sure it's clean. The sleeves are way too short, and my bony arms look like sticks on the sides of a snowman. I'm glad my sheets and pillowcase don't have to be "washed freshly" too, because I can't remember the last time we cleaned those!

I find some safety pins scattered around my desk; then I pin a bay leaf to each corner of my pillowcase. A few leaves break into a couple of pieces, but I'm not worried. I know the universe will understand my intention. I put a full leaf under the pillow as instructed, then go to put the dishes away.

As I walk down the hallway, I hear voices coming from the kitchen.

One is Dad's. The other is . . . a woman's!

Though I can't understand any words, I'm very glad not to hear Southern accents. I've had enough of those tonight. I stop and listen harder. This woman had better not be Paige. But I can't tell. I take a couple of steps closer, leaning forward, stretching my neck, still not hearing anything specific, leaning forward even more, until . . .

BANG! Something that sounds like a pot clangs against the floor or the counter. I scream! Then I fall over, right into the kitchen doorway, where Dad and whoever this woman is can see me from head to toe.

So much for trying to spy.

"Are you okay?" the woman asks, and finally I recognize her voice. I look up, and sure enough, it's Terri crouching down and leaning over me!

Though my call to Uncle Arnie was nothing but strange, maybe his postcard was right about taking a step! I only took the bay leaf bath five minutes ago, and here's Terri hanging out with my dad in the kitchen! I haven't even slept on my pillow yet, and the potion is already pushing Dad away from Paige. Yes!

"Terri, hi!" I say, probably too excited, as I stand up and fix my nightgown. "We already had dinner, but do you want some dessert? Our ice cream's kind of old and frosty, but Dad could go buy some."

"No, no," Dad says. "Terri's only here to get a pot she lent us."

A pot? Uh-oh. The last pot I used ended up in the trash.

"Why did you lend us a pot?" I ask.

"Your dad and I made beef bourguignonne, remember? And the pots you guys had here were . . ."

"Crummy," Dad says.

"But the beef bourguignonne was good," Terri says with a smile.

"What's beef blah-blah-blah?" I ask, not remembering a dinner with a name like that—a dinner that needed a special pot. A pot that no longer exists.

"We ate it over noodles. It's like a French beef stew." Terri takes in some short breaths. "It actually smells a little like . . ."

Dad sniffs too. "What *is* that smell?"

I'm not ready to answer that, so I scramble. "Just your darling daughter!"

"No, that's not it." He gets closer to me and breathes in deeply. "Were you playing with Toby in your room?"

"Um . . . yeah." At least I'm being honest there. I did pet Toby several times while I was typing up the potion.

"It's not skunk," Dad says, sniffing. "It's more like . . . stew."

I've got to wrap this up—and fast. "Oh well, I'll make

sure I shower before school. Good night, Dad. I'll put the dishes away in the morning." I kiss him on the cheek and zoom down the hallway, shouting, "Good to see you, Terri!" as I go.

"Wait!" Dad shouts. "Come here!"

I stop. I turn around slowly and go back. But I stand as far away as possible, on the other side of the doorway.

"I wanted to tell you: I looked up your uncle's quote," Dad says. "It's from Lao-tzu."

"Where's that?"

"It's not a place; it's a person. A Chinese philosopher."

That *is* pretty interesting, but as much as I'd like to spend time talking about Chinese philosophy and helping Dad and Terri get closer, right now I need to stay far away from their questioning noses. They haven't even started to talk about how red I am. That's bound to be next.

"That's cool, Dad. Thanks. See you in the morning. See you later, Terri!"

I wave. Terri waves back. And as I walk away, I hear her say, "That brother of yours is quite a character, isn't he?"

If only Terri knew!

I get to my room and jump into my bed. I want to fall right to sleep, but my mind is racing. Not only do I need to dream about Larry not liking me, I need to dream about Dad not liking Paige too. Kill two birds with one bay leaf bath, and everything will be solved!

All I have to do is fall asleep. It's what the potion says to do. But I still can't. My nose is filled with the smell of bay leaves. An hour or so ago, I didn't know what they were; now I'll never forget them.

My clock keeps tick-tick-ticking. This is getting serious now. I've got to fall asleep and I've got to dream . . . about the last people I want floating through my mind: Paige and Larry.

Eventually I fall asleep, and I dream for sure. There's a boy, but I don't think he's Larry because he has blond hair. Maybe it's Ryder Landry! I don't quite see his face, but he's wearing a knit beanie, so there's a good chance it's him. "Cleo, you're the girl for me," he says, taking my hand in his. I should be excited, but even in a dream I'm embarrassed. Then he lifts my hand to his lips and kisses it . . . or is he licking it? That's weird. And gross. Why is Ryder Landry licking my hand?

I open my eyes and look down my arm.

Ryder Landry isn't licking my hand.

Toby is!

I pull my hand away and give it a sniff. Yep, I still smell like bay leaves.

"Cleo, we're late!" Dad shouts from the front of the house.

Oh no! I jumped into bed so fast last night I forgot to

set the alarm. And Dad probably started reading again after Terri left and he fell asleep too!

As fast as I can, I hop from under my covers and hit the floor. "I have to take a shower!"

"No time!" Dad yells. I look at my clock and growl. He's right. It's way too late. "Throw on some clothes and let's go. I'll give you money for lunch!"

I pull on the first clothes I see and run to meet Dad at the car, hoping that lunch isn't stew today. I've had enough of that.

On our drive to school, we spot Red Shorts on a neighborhood street, reading his newspaper and walking quickly, as usual. Dad rolls down his window and says, "Beautiful day, huh?" Red Shorts nods, smiles without showing his teeth, and keeps walking.

"Does he ever stop?" I ask as Dad rolls up the window.

"I've never seen him stop," Dad says. "It's kind of a sad story, actually. At least from what I've heard. Who knows whether it's true or not."

"What?" I lean in. This could be interesting.

"Well, people say he and his wife used to walk together every once in a while. When she passed away, he couldn't stand being in his house alone, so he started to walk more and more, and now that's all he does."

I'm amazed. "He doesn't eat or sleep or go to the bathroom?"

Dad laughs. "He must do all that, but I don't know. All I know is that every time I see him, he's walking."

"Yeah, me too." It's hard to believe it's possible to love someone so much that it makes you walk and walk and walk. I don't like walking that much, so I'm fine if I never fall in love like that.

When Dad and I arrive at the parking lot at school, he surprises me by pulling into a space instead of stopping by the curb. Even worse, he takes off his seat belt!

"What are you doing?" I ask. It's bad enough to have your dad drop you off at school and for people to see if his hair is messy or he's wearing goofy glasses or he says something dumb like "Catch ya on the flip side," whatever that means. I don't want him *hanging out* here!

"I'm meeting a friend," he says—and then I see her. Paige! She's sitting on a bench by the entrance to the school, wearing her tight-fitting, expensive yoga pants and matching jacket. Lifting a large paper cup, most likely coffee, to her lips and taking a sip. Leaving a red lipstick stain, I'm sure, on its plastic lid. Dad can't possibly intend to stay and *sit* with her right in front of the school—can he? When Terri was just at our house last night?

I try to walk ahead, but Dad keeps the exact same pace

so we're walking together. Not cool. Then I see it—on the bench on the other side of Paige. *Another* cup of coffee!

A coffee date at your child's school? This is the worst parenting ever.

Terri would never do something so ridiculous. She knows better. She shows up for appropriate school events like plays and art shows—not dates.

"Have a good day," Dad says to me as he takes a seat with Paige.

"Nice to see you, Cleo," Paige says, her white teeth perfect, especially against that red lipstick, which is not smudged at all.

"Yeah, you too. Bye," I mumble, then zoom into the courtyard, hoping that no one has seen this offensive display. I stand outside our classroom door, scanning the room for Madison before I go in.

I feel a tap on my shoulder. "*What* is going on in front of the school?" I'm startled at first, but it's exactly who I was hoping to see.

"Oh my gosh, Madison, thank goodness. We have *got* to talk—"

She interrupts. "What is that smell?"

So it didn't fade at all on the way to school. Great.

"It's a potion I made last night, trying to reverse everything."

Madison's eyes get big and bright. "Did you use your love potion? Finally?"

"No, I didn't," I tell her, "but I really, really wanted to." She laughs when I tell her about calling Uncle Arnie and the wacky lady at his house, and about my hot and stinky bay leaf bath. "I guess it *was* kind of funny," I admit, "but it didn't work. Dad still likes Samantha's mom. At least enough to have a coffee date. Yuck."

Madison looks thoughtful. "Well . . . is that really so bad?" she asks.

Why would she say such a thing? She knows the plan! Dad and *Terri*.

Madison leans in. "Does it really matter who your dad falls in love with, as long as he's in love and not so sad anymore?"

I can understand why she thinks that. But I know how it's wrong, and I know exactly how to explain it to her. "It's like that Ryder Landry song," I say. *"You don't want just anyone. You only want your only one. The one who always stuns, the one who never runs, the one who's there for fun. The one who will be by your side forever . . ."*

Madison joins in. *"The one who will turn on you never, never ever . . ."* She waves her hand in front of me. "Stop. I'm going to cry." It's true; her eyes are a little bit watery. "Are you sure Terri is your dad's *Only One*?"

"For sure!" I say. "How could I go on with my life, all normal, when I know that he's supposed to be with her but ended up with Sam's mom because of me? I mean, I tried to make that happen once and I'm sorry I did. He didn't like

Paige then and he *can't* like her now. They don't look right together. They don't *sound* right together. They don't have fun conversations and jokes. She's just . . . *there*."

"Well then, we've got to get him together with Terri," says Madison.

I agree. That's where he belongs.

She's definitely his *Only One*.

13

Before we can discuss it further, the bell rings. School's always getting in the way of more important things. I rush to my seat, and though I don't mean to, I glance toward Larry.

He's looking straight at me, raising his eyebrows in a long-distance hello. If eyebrows could talk, they'd be saying, "*I love you.*"

This isn't good.

I turn away as quickly as possible, as Kevin tells us to get out our math workbooks. I pull my pencil case out of my desk and open it.

POP! KA-BLOW! An explosion of colorful confetti flies into the air, into my hair, onto my clothes, and then onto the floor. Lisa Lee screams like she's heard a gunshot, and Kylie Mae puts her hand over her heart. They're both being

a little dramatic. I mean, this was surprising, but it was hardly heart-attack surprising!

Picking the confetti out of my hair, I see that it's shaped like stars, hearts, and smiley faces. It's got to be Larry. He's definitely the kind of boy who could rig a mini explosion inside a pencil case; plus his lovey-eyebrow face has turned into a goofy, grinning one. The little monkey on his desk looks like he's smiling too, though I know in reality he always has the same expression.

I glance at Samantha, praying she doesn't have any idea where this romantic gesture came from. She has no expression at all—but I hope her expressionless expression isn't anger. I know what she does when she's angry: she chases you through graveyards and throws boots and pepperoni at you!

Kevin, however, is not expressionless. "Cleo, what's this all about? What is this mess?"

"It wasn't me!" I sputter. But here I am, covered in the stuff. There's no denying I'm involved somehow.

"Well, clean it up when we have our next break. Let's turn to page one-eighty-two and get started. . . ."

I look over at Madison. She understands what's going on and feels my pain. Larry's half nodding, like he wants my approval. He's not going to get it.

Well, if I had any question about the bay leaf potion before, I don't now. It hasn't worked.

The day gets worse from there.

At lunchtime, Madison says she's hungrier than usual, but I'm guessing that's because I smell like stew. We stand in the lunch line together. Normally I wouldn't buy lunch on the day they serve almond-encrusted organic chicken breast and steamed garlic spinach, but today I have no choice, since Dad didn't make me a lunch.

As a cafeteria worker puts a rice cake on my tray (we get those instead of rolls, which might actually be tasty), I hear a voice behind me. "What's that smell?"

It's Lisa Lee, looking like someone's holding a week-old bologna sandwich under her nose. "Are you *wearing* your lunch?"

"She smells like my mom's spice rack," Kylie Mae whispers, loud enough for me to hear, of course.

"Maybe it's the latest perfume," Madison tells them.

I like that idea! I add, "Yeah, it's so new, you don't even know about it." Los Angeles is odd enough that this could maybe be true. Dad told me he heard about a restaurant where people eat dinner in a pitch-black room, and they can't see their food or their forks or even their hands in front of their faces. In LA, any weird thing can be popular.

Lisa Lee and Kylie Mae look at each other. For a moment—one tiny, hopeful moment—it looks like they could possibly, just possibly, believe me. Then they both shake their heads. "Nah," they agree.

Oh well. We tried.

I step away from them to pay the cashier. I know I have my wallet in my backpack, but I'm not sure which pocket it's in, so I have to unzip them all. The cashier sighs as I hear the conversation behind me.

"I really hope you'll come to the Bling Bling with us," says Lisa Lee.

Kylie Mae adds her usual, "Yeah."

Then I hear Madison's voice. "I'm not sure. We'll see."

We'll see? I try to concentrate on finding my wallet, but it's kind of hard when I'm hearing this.

"Come on, Maddy, we've been doing it all our lives, and we always have the best time; you know it's true." I wonder if Madison hears the same whiny voice I do when I listen to Lisa Lee.

"Yeah," Kylie Mae says again.

Madison says she doesn't know. "I'll think about it. I'll be seeing you this summer anyway."

"That's why we need to kick it off at the Bling Bling, duh!" says Lisa Lee.

"Yeah," Kylie Mae says. "Duh."

The more I listen, the more disturbed I get. Then, finally, I pull out my wallet, trying to feel triumphant instead of bummed. I give the cashier a weak smile, but she's not impressed by the magnificent feat of finding my money.

"Um, you dropped something," says Lisa Lee. I can tell by the tone of her voice that she's not talking to Madison anymore.

When I turn, Kylie Mae is bending down and picking up a piece of paper from the floor. I have no idea what it is, but I'm sure I don't want Kylie Mae's mitts on it! She hands it to Lisa Lee, who unfolds it.

"Hey, that's Cleo's!" says Madison. But it's too late.

Lisa Lee reads it out loud. *"You, you, you plus me, me, me. Put them together and it's fun at the Bling Bling Summer Fling."* She looks up from the paper. "Someone's a Ryder Landry fan, I see."

Of course I know who it's from, and he's the opposite of a Ryder Landry fan. He's just making a chemistry joke.

"Who's it from?" Kylie Mae asks.

"Doesn't say," says Lisa Lee. Thank goodness! If he had written *Love, Larry* (or something crazier, like *Lovingly yours* or *Your one true love*), I would never hear the end of it. Lisa Lee folds the note back up and hands it to me. "But it looks like you have a date to the Bling Bling. So you won't mind if Madison comes with us."

The cashier clears her throat. She's been waiting a long time for her money.

"That's, um, up to Madison," I say.

"She does smell funny," I hear Kylie Mae say as I pay the cashier and flee into the lunchroom. I scan the room from side to side and don't see Larry. I'm glad. If he got close enough to get a whiff of me, he'd probably say I smell as nice as a powdery baby or an ice cream parlor serving waffle cones.

I gobble up my food, barely even talking to Madison. I don't want to discuss her plans for the Bling Bling Summer Fling, and I don't want to run into Larry. I just want to force down my organic chicken breast and steamed spinach and get back to class.

When Larry walks into the lunchroom with his tray, I'm done. "I'm gonna go," I tell Madison, standing up and heading toward the door.

I've only been under the jungle gym for a minute when Madison runs out to join me. "You can't live like this the rest of your life!" she says, a little out of breath.

"I know," I agree. "We have to do something. Something that will work."

Madison looks sympathetic. "Okay, then, let's do another potion. As soon as possible."

"Why?" I ask. "Because the other ones have worked out so great?" I know I should try to be positive, but I can't help it. We were only trying to do something good, and now it's a big mess—with me in the middle. Smelling like stew.

"What other choice do we have?" asks Madison. "Look, we don't know exactly what's going on with your dad and Sam's mom, but this one with you and Larry—we've got to fix that!"

Of course Madison is right. A love potion caused it; a love potion is going to have to make it right.

When Kevin tells us it's time for the Focus! kids to head to Focus!, my heart feels paralyzed. I don't want to walk across the schoolyard with Larry, so I leap from my chair and run for the door. I pull it open so fast, it almost hits me in the face. I cross the lawn, hearing Larry call out, "Hey, wait up!" but I pretend like I'm too far away to hear and zoom into the Focus! room, pushing other kids out of the way to keep my distance.

Roberta has moved all the desks and chairs to the edges of the room, and I'm hoping this means we'll play improvisational games, like when we tried out for *Healthyland*. Working on the play, it was acceptable to be weird. When you're an actor, it might even be acceptable to smell like bay leaves. I bet Johnny Depp smells like bay leaves all the time.

When all the other kids have streamed into the room—and I spot Larry and Samantha on the opposite side—Roberta announces what we'll be doing today. Unfortunately, it's not improv games. It's something scary.

Not scary like bungee jumping from a high tower or eating rat intestines or anything, but pretty darn scary for a random day at Friendship Community School.

Square dancing. Ugh!

I saw square dancing once at a county fair. A bunch of

old couples, probably married a million years, were wearing what looked like Wild West costumes and walking around in circles to corny music. Square dancing is all about twirling and bowing and skipping around. This isn't education; this is torture!

"Square dancing is a great way to practice listening, following instructions, and working together," Roberta tells everyone. She walks around the room and pulls people into position on the empty floor. "Plus, it's fun," she adds, though if the county fair was any example, I doubt it!

Roberta puts Larry in the middle of the room and goes to get him a partner. I hunch my shoulders and hold my head down.

"Roberta, I know who my partner should be," Larry says in a big, grand manner. It scares me.

It should.

"Come on, Cleo. We're partners in chemistry. Let's be partners in square dancing too!"

I wish I could drink a potion right now and shrink to the size of a cockroach. I'd skitter across the floor, underneath the door, and out into the yard and burrow into the ground, as far down into the dirt as I could go.

I look to Roberta as if she could save me, but she gestures for me to get up there while she places other people in position. Larry bows, which I might have found funny on any other day, but *now—today—*it's horrible. What if Lisa

Lee and Kylie Mae were here to see this? They thought his stupid *note* was hilarious, and this is a million billion times more embarrassing!

Then it gets worse: I look at Samantha and she's staring at her sneakers like they hold the clue to something really important, like world peace or the best chocolate chip cookie recipe ever. When Roberta walks toward her, Sam looks up and says—with her voice all weak and wounded, a way she never sounds—that she hurt her ankle and can't do physical activity.

But I know the truth.

I hope she doesn't think I had anything to do with this. I hope she thinks Larry is just being his usual goofy self, not that he's declaring me his partner in life or anything. I look closely at her to see if I can get any sense—any little hint—of how she's feeling, but her face is blank. When Samantha was my best friend, I always knew how she felt, at least until she turned against me. I wish I could understand what's going on now.

Roberta actually lets her sit on the sidelines, making me wish I'd thought of this excuse first. This is another reason I need to be friends with Sam again. She's quick and smart. I could use those smarts right about now.

But instead I've got to square dance. With Larry.

Roberta starts teaching us the dance moves, and almost all of them include the last thing in the world I want to do right now—holding hands! Sure, the boy just puts his palm up and the girl puts her hand on top of it, but . . . yuck.

I'm holding hands.

With a boy who wants to be my partner in more than chemistry! With a boy whose hand has a little bit of nervous moisture on it. Now, I don't want to be rude about Larry, because my hand is sweaty too. Even worse, the smell of bay leaves is coming out of my hand . . . and my armpits . . . and the area under my nose. I'm a big, sweaty beef bourguignonne, holding hands with a boy.

As we promenade left (which means walking in a circle back to our original position), Larry asks, "Are you wearing perfume or something?"

"Sort of," I tell him. Like I'm really going to explain my bay leaf bath while I'm do-si-do-ing, which means facing your partner and then circling around him like a goofball until you're facing him again. How is this entertainment? This dance must have been invented to ruin kids' lives.

"I like it," he says as we link arms and swing around in a circle. "It smells earthy."

Earthy? Well, if Larry were my boyfriend, I certainly would not appreciate that compliment. Then again, what else could he say? I don't smell like daffodils or an ocean breeze or lavender air freshener.

I think about how fun this could have been on an ordinary day, when Larry and I were ordinary friends. When we were *only* friends. If I had taken the bay leaf bath for any other reason, I might have told him all about it, and we would have laughed. But no, when love enters the picture, you can't be free and natural and tell the boy what you really think. Not when he's acting like this!

Ryder Landry is probably the only boy who knows how to act around a girl. He might be the one person on Earth who could make square dancing cool. But unfortunately, he's nowhere to be found. I didn't get to read any of the Lander websites this morning, but he's probably packing for his tour of Asia.

Nineteen hours later—at least that's what it feels like—Roberta says we're going to wrap up by bowing and curtsying to our partners. "Thanks, Cleo. That was fun," Larry says. At least I think that's what he says. I'm running to the other side of the room and out the door as fast as I can. Samantha is close behind, pretending to hobble for the first couple of steps, then walking normally once she's safely out of the Focus! room.

"Hey, is something going on with you and Larry?" she asks me.

Oh no! She's onto us! Her voice is trying to sound casual, but this is Samantha, after all. There's always more to it.

"It's a long story," I say, still walking ahead of her.

"There's something weird going on! I know it!" she shouts after me.

I want to talk to Samantha; I'd love to explain everything

and try to be friends again, but today is not the day. Not until I've had a chance to put an end to the Cleo-Larry love story.

Because of the Bling Bling Summer Fling assembly yesterday, we have Recreational Wellness today. I usually don't like running around and sweating in front of other kids, but who cares anymore? At least it means school is almost over, and afterward I can finally go home and stop smelling like bay leaves and be far, far away from the loving eyes of Larry, the judging eyes of Lisa Lee and Kylie Mae, and the questioning eyes of Samantha.

I'm even a little relieved when Janet announces that today's game will be kickball. It's nowhere near as terrible as field hockey or doing push-ups or playing crab soccer. I'm actually not bad at kicking that red rubber ball. I've even gotten on base a couple of times.

And I'm a *lot* relieved when Janet puts Larry on the other team. Unfortunately, Madison is called to be on that team too, along with her Bling Bling pals Lisa Lee and Kylie Mae, and I find myself sitting on the bench next to Samantha, waiting to kick.

"I know what you guys are up to," she says to me out of the blue. Sam can zero in on things that no one else notices, then shock you with a comment like that when you least expect it.

"What are you talking about?" I ask, only halfway between playing dumb and being dumb.

"Madison told me all about it at the art show."

That's strange. If Madison said anything to Sam about the love potion, she would've told me about it . . . wouldn't she? Unless she was really embarrassed for telling our secret. Then she might not.

But I doubt she did.

Of course she didn't. No way. So I tell Sam, "She did not."

"Yeah, she did. But she said it didn't work." Sam gives me a shrug, like *What can you do?*

I shrug back. Then, luckily, it's time for me to kick. The ball goes straight to Ronnie Cheseboro, who's playing first base, so I'm out. Lisa Lee, who's playing second base, squeals and cheers for her boyfriend. I don't really care whether I get on base or not; I'm just happy to be sitting back at the end of the line, far from Sam.

Until Sam gets tagged out too, and she's back next to me. "I didn't want to get on base anyway," Samantha says. "Who wants more running?"

"Yeah, especially with your *bad ankle*," I comment, but Sam doesn't have much reaction. She just sniffs slightly and jumps back in with another question.

"So what are you going to do next?"

"About what?" I'm still trying to play innocent, but I'm not sure how long I can pull it off.

Misunderstanding." There is so much going on in my life right now, and Ryder knows how hard it is to be a kid. That's what this song is all about.

> *They laugh at us, they say we're cute.*
> *They don't understand, it's hard for me and you.*
> *Life's not easy, we know that's true.*
> *They don't understand, it's hard for me and you.*

As I listen, I leaf through the potion book, looking at its illustrations and wondering which recipe to make next. I don't want to pick one, translate it, and then find out it doesn't fit the problem I have with me and Larry and Dad and Terri and Paige. Ryder keeps on singing:

> *We don't know what to do, we don't know how*
> *   to do it.*
> *Grown-ups don't understand, they just tell us*
> *   how we blew it . . .*

DING! There's a text message on my phone. It's from Madison.

Can you talk?

Sure, I write back. What about?

Call me.

Wow. I barely ever talk to Madison on the phone. Why would I ever talk to anyone on the phone when there's texting? But I dial her number and hear one ring. Madison answers right away. "I have something to tell you," she says. "I've been meaning to for days, and when I saw you and Samantha talking at kickball, I realized . . ."

"I know," I tell her.

"You know?"

"I know you didn't tell her everything, but she figured out most of it. Then she tricked me into telling her."

Madison seems happy to finally tell the truth. Sam was grilling her mercilessly at the art show, and Madison only got away because her parents interrupted. "That was the first time I was ever happy to see my parents," she says with a laugh. "But Sam probably would've broken me down if she'd had a few more minutes. She was like a squirrel with a nut."

"Yep, she's like a dog with a bone," I say, picturing her face on Toby's body. Sam's got her teeth in Toby's favorite pork chop–shaped chew toy, and she won't let go no matter how hard I pull at it.

"Listen, we know things can go wrong. This is all about making them right again," says Madison. "Let's invite Sam over to my house after school this week, and she can help us pick a potion."

"She does know Spanish," I say.

"And if she wants to do a love potion because she likes Larry, that will solve *your* little problem," Madison points out.

I'm liking this idea more and more. "Are you sure?"

"Sure," she says, like it's no big deal.

Wow. I bet Samantha never expected she'd be invited to Madison Paddington's mansion . . . but then again, I never did either!

We say goodbye, and I put Ryder's song back on. The final triumphant lyrics of "Understanding Misunderstanding" put me in a better mood. With Ryder, anything seems possible:

> *One day they will trust us, we'll climb that hill . . .*
> *They don't understand now, but . . . but someday they willlllllllll!*

14

Madison does some quick planning, and a couple of texts later, everything's been arranged. The next day after school, Yvonne the au pair picks the three of us up in the Paddingtons' SUV, and we're off to Madison's.

Samantha is unusually quiet as we open the giant wooden front doors, walk over the marble floors in the entryway, climb the big curved steps to the second floor, and head down the wide hallway to Madison's bedroom. "This is the life," Sam whispers to me. "I wish she had a brother!"

"Why? Do you like boys now?" I ask. I know the answer is yes, of course, and I know exactly who she likes, but I keep hoping I can get her to admit it.

"That's a personal question." Things are never easy with Sam.

"Well, we're about to pick a love potion together, so why wouldn't I ask?" If she's doing a potion for herself and Larry, then I won't have to do a spell to get him to stop loving me! I can concentrate totally on Dad and Terri.

"Why? Is there someone you like?" she asks. "Larry?"

Ha! I knew if I set the trap, she'd mention him at some point. "No!" I tell her. "I mean, yeah, I *like* Larry, but as a friend."

"What's wrong with him?"

"Nothing," I say, and I mean it. "He's awesome. Why? Do *you* like him?"

Samantha doesn't reply immediately. This little pause might be my answer! I look closely at her face. Her mouth is about to open. She's about to tell me the truth. And the truth is . . .

"Here's my room!" Madison announces, opening her door. Darn it! Sam's attention becomes ultra-focused on the bedroom. She takes it all in, from floor to ceiling, from left to right. She probably feels like I did the first time I saw it—like she's stepped into a fairy tale.

"Where does that go?" she asks, pointing at the shuttered doors leading to the patio. Madison opens them and we all walk onto the balcony overlooking the yard and pool. The greens and blues below us are so bright, they look like they've been run through some kind of filter on the computer.

"Oh, wow, we should've gone swimming!" Samantha groans. She has a nice pool at her condo building, but not like Madison's. There may not be *actual* diamonds sparkling on top of the crystal-blue water down there, but it sure looks like it!

"Next time," says Madison. "Let's go inside; we've got a lot to do."

Sam and I walk back in together, Samantha mouthing *Next time* with a smile.

We settle on Madison's clean wood floor. I open my backpack and pull out *POCIÓNES FANTÁSTICOS.* I hand it to Samantha, who doesn't look very impressed. "Wow, this is *ancient,*" she says. "Why are you using this weird old book when your uncle sent you a love potion?"

"That's what *I* keep asking!" Madison says.

I groan. "Because he hasn't told me how it works. Sam, we had *instructions* for the voodoo doll, and that was a big, fat mess."

"Yeah, I guess," she says, "but . . ."

I cross my arms over my chest. "I'm not even going to let you try to convince me. I haven't used the love potion yet, and I won't. Not until I know how it works."

Samantha looks at Madison and lets out a whistle. "Okay, then." She rolls her eyes a little like I'm being silly, but I can't let her change my mind. I nod my head once, firmly, and Samantha looks down to open the book.

I can't believe my tough act worked! Yay!

Sam opens the book to a random yellowed page and reads for a moment. Now she looks interested, and she seems to understand what she's seeing. "Ooh," she says, looking at one potion. I lean over to see what it is, but she turns the page.

"Ahhh," she says, looking at the next one. Other sounds follow: *hmmm, ohhhh,* a chuckle, *huhhh,* and a snort.

I can't stand it anymore! "Stop making noises and tell us which one we should do!"

"Okay, I have a couple of ideas . . . ," Samantha begins. But that's when an intercom buzzes and Yvonne's voice fills Madison's room.

"Maddy, your cookies are ready. But I need to prepare for our homework session tonight, so you'll have to come get them yourself."

Madison looks at us and sighs a little. Then she shrugs, stands up, and says, "I'll be right back."

As soon as she's gone, Samantha leans in to me. "I think normally the cookies *come to her!*"

"Yeah," I say. "Their chef sometimes brings us snacks up here."

"Their *chef?*" Sam seems in shock. "This," she says, gesturing around the room, "is not our lives."

I agree.

"But, I mean, it will *never* be our lives," Sam says.

"It's nice to visit, though!" I say, smiling.

"Yeah, I guess." Sam looks like she has deeper thoughts on her mind. "Listen, you're new here. You don't know LA. I know Madison seems nice and all right now, but girls like her never stick with girls like us. We're fun to have around for a while because we're interesting and different, but when you live a life like this, Cleo, you're living in another world. We *do not* fit in."

"I don't know why not," I tell her. "I was picturing spending the whole summer out at the pool with cookies and fresh lemonade and—"

"Well, that's not going to happen." Samantha's voice doesn't sound mean—just . . . truthful. "Everyone knows Madison goes to Hawaii all summer, and her *best friends* Lisa Lee and Kylie Mae go too."

"Yeah, but she doesn't like them so much right now—" I start to say.

"I don't know. They all looked pretty happy onstage the other day."

Samantha's right. At the Bling Bling assembly, Madison, Lisa Lee, and Kylie Mae looked . . . *perfect* together. Ryder Landry says there's *Only One* special person to love. I wonder if there's only a certain number of important friends too. Am I one of Madison's?

Samantha's still talking. "We might as well have as much fun as possible until the Bling Bling Summer Fling, because after that, it's summer. And when it's summer, Madison's going to say 'Adios, Cleo.' You know what that means?"

I glare at her. "Yes, I know what *adios* means."

Madison walks into the room, and I'm happy to have a reason to shut up. I don't want these days of fresh-baked cookies and freezing-cold milk on silver trays to end. Not only because Madison's got an au pair and an awesome house and a fantastic pool, but because I *like* Madison. I like having more than one friend! I don't want to lose another one. Like Jane Anne. Like Samantha.

Sam jumps to her feet, grabs a cookie, and chomps into it. "Oh my gosh, they're still warm!" With her mouth full, she adds, "Deee-licious!"

All talk stops as we sit on the floor with the tray in the middle. For a few minutes, the only sounds are slurps, gulps, and the occasional *yum, num,* or *mmmm.* But when the cookies are gone, it's time to get down to business.

"So, did you pick a potion?" Madison asks, shoving the tray to the side and bringing *POCIÓNES FANTÁSTICOS* back between us.

"I found one I like," Sam tells us. "But it's not really a potion. It's more like a charm."

"That might be better," I say. "Getting the right people to drink a potion is pretty tough." And taking a bath in one isn't a blast either, though I don't say that out loud.

Samantha opens the book to a page titled *LLAMADA DE LA SIRENA.*

"Isn't *llamada* like a phone call?" asks Madison.

"*Sí, señorita,*" says Samantha. Then she reads us the charm.

"THE CALL OF THE SIREN.
In mythology, sailors who heard the song of the beautiful
female sirens were mesmerized by their voices and would

crash into the rocky coast. This siren's call will send your mesmerizing voice to the universe, and your bidding will be done. If there is someone you love, you may call that person to you. If there is someone you do not love, you may send that person away. Would you like to bring two perfect loves together? Just ask the universe with your unique and exquisite siren call."

"Exquisite?" Madison asks.

"*Exquisito,*" says Samantha. "That must be what it means."

"Let's not worry too much about the adjectives," I say, excited to hear the rest. "What do we have to *do?*"

"Well, lucky you, that's what's next," Sam says, and keeps reading.

"First, you will take a seashell to a body of water, such as a river, lake, or ocean. The choice of water may be yours. As you scoop up some water with the shell, sing a verse of your favorite love song. The universe must hear your call, so your voice must be loud and strong with no dudas."

Madison laughs. "Doo-doos?"

That's so dumb that I have to giggle too. "I'll definitely try not to have doo-doos while I'm singing."

Sam looks up, realizing she didn't translate the word.

"Oh, right! Ummm, *dudas* are . . . doubts. No doubts. No, um, hesitations."

"Cool, no problem," I say. I poke my finger back at the book. "What else, what else?"

Sam finds her place on the page and continues.

> *"Place the shell on a string and make a necklace. It may circle your neck, or the neck of the person for whom you make your wish. Wear it with pride, positivity, and happiness. When it falls off, your wish for yourself or another will come true."*

"Okay, that doesn't sound too bad," says Madison.

"Hold your horses," Sam tells her. "That's not the end." She keeps reading.

> *"In exchange for the cleansing water you have taken from the earthly world, leave behind an offering. This offering should be an extension of the person for whom you are calling the universe. Be fearless, sweet sirens, and make your calls. The universe will listen. It has ear canals large."*

We laugh, and Sam realizes her translation mistake. "The universe has large ear canals," she says, then finishes reading.

"However, a warning! Do not share your wishes with others. Your calls are for the ear canals of the universe only."

Samantha looks up at us. "How does that sound?"

It sounds okay to me, I guess. Madison already knows what I want to do for Dad and Terri and Larry and Sam, but the universe can't be mad at me for sharing that stuff before I knew I shouldn't . . . right?

The good news is that we can ask the universe for pretty much anything, as long as we sing the right song, leave the right offering, and don't discuss it with other people. Still, this is going to be complicated for me. I wish this could be a project for Focus! class, because I've got a lot to accomplish in a short time, and I'm going to need to do a lot of the things Roberta teaches us: assess my situation, list my needs, budget my time, and follow through to reach my goals.

The thing is: I need to ask the universe for a *lot* of stuff.

First of all, Dad and Terri. It might be hard to explain to Dad why I want him to wear some ratty piece of string with a shell on it, but if I say it's important to me, he'll do it. Parents have to do those kinds of dumb things when they love their children.

Next up, Larry. He needs to like Samantha instead of me. So that means I need to get an "offering" from him, then get him to wear a necklace too. How do I do all that without him thinking that I *like* him? That one's going to take longer to figure out.

Finally, I decide that I'll wear a necklace too. I don't know if the *LLAMADA DE LA SIRENA* can guarantee that two friends stay together, but if Samantha's right, Madison might not be my friend much longer.

Uncle Arnie once taught me that friendship is the meeting of love and magic. So if friendship equals magic plus love, then a magic (spell) plus a love (potion book) could equal friendship. Right? It's simple math!

It's a lot to do, and I've got one day to do it. Because we decide that Saturday, the day after tomorrow, is the day we'll call the universe from the lake across from my house. And I need to be ready.

As soon as Yvonne drops me off at home, I get to work. First on my list is to find an "offering" for Dad, but I have no idea where to start. What is an "extension" of him? Toby, probably, but I can't throw him in the lake!

While Dad's cooking dinner, I nose around his bedroom. There are clothes on the floor, in his hamper, and hanging in his closet. But everyone has clothes, and Dad's never treated anything like it's special. He's also got tons of books. They're in his bed, on his dresser, and piled on the floor. He reads a lot, but I wouldn't know which exact book is an extension of him—though I do wish he'd read

Quantum Physics, Biocentrism, and the Universe as We Know It and do a report on it for me!

I go into Dad's dining room office. He's always sitting at his computers, but they're expensive and important to his work, so I'm definitely not touching those.

"Are you looking for something?" Dad asks from the kitchen.

At that moment, way on the back of his desk, behind a stack of file folders and an old trophy from a softball league in Ohio, I see a pair of his glasses. He used to wear them all the time. The lenses are thick and they have roundish black frames. "Kind of," I say, fishing out the glasses from the mess. One of the arms is missing. "I wanted to draw one of my characters wearing glasses, so I was going to borrow yours." And now that I think of it, Pandaroo *would* look good in glasses!

Dad comes over to take a closer look. "Oh, you can have those," he says. "They're broken."

"Why didn't you throw them out?" I ask, placing them over my eyes. They immediately go lopsided because of the missing arm.

"What do I ever throw out?" he asks, and we both laugh because we have that in common. "I don't know why they're still here," he says, heading back to the kitchen. "Maybe because Terri liked them. She called me the Owl when I wore those."

"Does Terri like your new glasses?" I ask.

"I don't know; I haven't asked her."

"Oh." I don't know what else to say. But I know these glasses should be my offering to the universe for Dad. They're missing an arm, and Dad is missing Terri. These glasses remind him of her, and she liked him wearing them.

"It was nice to see Terri the other night," I say to Dad. I know I'll be asking the universe to do the work, but it doesn't hurt to get *him* thinking more about Terri too. "Why did she come over for her pot?"

Back in the kitchen, stirring noodles in one of our old, rusty pots, Dad says he doesn't know.

"Was she making dinner for someone?" I ask. "Like a new boyfriend?"

Dad laughs. "I'm not sure, Cleo. Not that I know of."

"So she wouldn't know if you had a new girlfriend?"

Dad laughs again. "No. But that's something I probably wouldn't mention to her either."

Darn! That would have been the perfect opportunity for him to tell me about his new girlfriend—if Paige *is* his new girlfriend—but he's still keeping it secret. I'm sure if Samantha were having this conversation, she would have a sneaky way to get the information, but I'm not so devious. I'm just going to ask him what I really want to know.

"Dad," I ask seriously, "do you ever miss Terri?"

Dad doesn't even pause to think. "Sure," he says.

"Do you think there's one true love for everybody?"

He turns off the stove and moves the pot of noodles to the sink. "That's a pretty tough question," Dad says. "Why do you ask?"

"I don't know," I say. "Sometimes I wonder if Mom was your one true love. Or if you think there's another one out there." Of course what I'm really thinking is, *Paige had better not be your next true love. Terri is!*

"Why are you asking these questions?" Dad asks. "You don't like a boy, do you?"

"No!" I say. "No, no, no, no, no!" Then I think about it. "Except Ryder Landry, I guess."

Dad rolls his eyes. "Oh, *that* kid?" I can tell he wants to make fun of Ryder, but he controls himself. "The . . . singer?"

"Yeah. He's so cute and smart and cool, and he can sing and he can write. Dad, you really should listen to his songs; he knows a lot about life and love and—"

"Yeah, that's okay," Dad says. He's finished with the noodles and it's time for dinner. "I don't need to take love advice from a teenager."

"He's not . . ." I stop myself. "Never mind." Dad's right; he doesn't have to take love advice from a teenager. He's going to do what his eleven-year-old—and the universe— decides is right for him.

15

Another morning at Friendship Community School, another disappointment.

When Dad pulls the car into the parking lot, Paige is there, with two coffees, on her bench. *Their* bench.

"Doesn't she have a job?" I ask as Dad and I get out of the car. Dad's look tells me how rude he thinks that was. "I'm only asking because she has a lot of time for coffee." That's a good explanation, right?

"Her job's a little like mine; she works with different clients on her own time."

I'm sorry I mentioned it. Of all the things I don't care about in the world, Paige's job is close to the top of the list. So I just say, "Oh," and then "See ya, Dad," and I head toward school. I take one more look as Dad sits next to Paige on the bench and she hands him something that looks like a scrapbook or photo album. He opens it and looks inside, and they start to talk. Oh yippee, they're sharing precious memories now.

Only one more day until the Siren Call. Thank goodness.

When it's time for chemistry, I don't feel the usual excitement of Ryder Landry singing *you, you, you plus me, me, me.* Today in class, I've got a goal that will mean the difference between success and failure with my Siren Call. And it's going to be a lot harder than getting a pair of old glasses from Dad.

Though I've done my best to avoid Larry the last few days, when we push our desks together and he puts out Mono the monkey, I'm as friendly and smiley as his old pal Cleo used to be. Meanwhile, at the front of the room, Kevin tells us that today's experiment is going to show us how some things can be a liquid and a solid at the same time.

"Like diarrhea!" cracks Lonnie Cheseboro. His brother laughs, but Lisa Lee and Kylie Mae are not amused. For once, I'm in agreement with them.

Kevin sighs. "No. Not like that," he says. "Sometimes a liquid, when moved a certain way, becomes a solid, and vice versa." He has the chemistry teams come to the front of the room to pick up bowls full of cornstarch, which he explains is used for thickening up liquids in cooking and stuff. Then we need to go to the sink and mix it with water to see what happens next.

"You want to mix first?" Larry asks.

I look down at the watery yellow mixture, remembering the bucket of papier-mâché Madison used to make her Ryder head. I gulp. "How about you start?"

He plunges his hands in with no problem at all. "Do you see how it's becoming more and more solid as you knead it?" Kevin asks as he walks around the room. "The molecules are being forced into the middle of each grain of powder because of the pressure you're putting on it."

Sure enough, the cornstarch looks like it's turning into a blob of clay right before my eyes. Now I have no problem checking it out. Kevin tells us we can even punch the mixture. When I do, it feels hard. I punch it again and it even cracks a little!

"Hey, take it easy!" Larry jokes. "What'd this cornstarch ball ever do to you?"

I laugh and hand it back to him. When our hands touch, I pull back quickly. Laughing together might be okay, but touching is definitely *not* good, especially with Samantha just across the classroom! Which reminds me of my other, more important goal for today's chemistry class—getting Larry's monkey. And I'm going to have to do it soon.

Kevin tells us to put the blob back into the bowl, and that's when a magical—or chemical—thing happens. It goes back to being a liquid! When Larry puts his hand in and lifts it up, the mixture falls through his fingers. "That's cool," I say.

"You gotta try it."

"Ewww, no, I can't."

"Yes you can! Deep down you have a sense of adventure, and this is adventurous. It's like playing in quicksand!"

Larry's right. And he doesn't know half the adventures I've had. If I can take a bath in bay leaves and not know what's going to happen, why can't I do this?

I grit my teeth and plunge a hand in. It's actually not as gross and clammy as Madison's papier-mâché. Larry lifts up his monkey to take a look. "All right!" he says. "Mono is proud of you!"

This is it! Larry has given me the perfect opening. It's time to do what I came here to do, no matter how tough it's going to be. "I'm glad he liked it," I say. I lean over like I'm talking to the little monkey. "Have you ever seen anything like that where you're from?" Then I look up at Larry. "Where is he from again?"

"Costa Rica," he says. "In Central America."

"That's so cool!" I say, looking at the monkey more closely. He's almost smiling and has a little mischief in his tiny eyes. He really is cute. But more importantly, he's an *extension of who Larry is.* Mono will make the Siren Call work, and after that, Larry will like Samantha instead of me!

As Larry and I empty our gunk into a trash can and return the bowl to Kevin, it's finally time to make my move.

"Do you think I could take him home for the weekend? I'd love to show him to my dad."

"I don't know," he says, looking uncertain. "Maybe instead I could show Mono to your dad in the parking lot when he picks you up."

Darn it! Why is Larry so smart? "Yeah, that would be great . . . ," I say, stalling for time. "But, you know what, my uncle Arnie is coming to town on Sunday, and he's the one who would really love it." I catch myself saying the word *love* and I stop for a second. But I have to go on. "He's always wanted to visit Costa Rica because he . . ." I can't say the word *love* again. "He likes monkeys so much."

"I don't know," Larry says again, and I'm afraid I'm going to lose this battle. For one terrible second, I actually think about stealing Mono. But I can't. No matter how awkward Larry has made my life for the last couple of days, I couldn't do that.

Larry picks up the monkey and looks at it. "I haven't been away from this monkey in a long time," he says. "But you know what? I'm a man. I can handle it. You're my friend, Cleo. I . . . like you."

He took a pause before *like*. I'm sure he was thinking *love,* but I'm so glad he didn't say it.

Then Larry hands me the monkey.

"Oh my gosh, thanks so much!" I wrap my hand around Mono's little body and I can feel all the delicate carving against my fingers. "I can't believe . . . I mean, my uncle's going to be so excited. Thanks, Larry!"

I'm so happy, I do the dumbest thing possible. With the entire class wandering around, cleaning their desks and washing their bowls, I hug Larry.

Larry steps back, surprise shooting out of his eyes. I step back even farther. I'm the one who did it, but I'm even more shocked than he is. Across the room, Samantha looks sour. I want to run over to her and explain how this is all a mis- understanding and the only reason I hugged Larry was because he gave me his monkey, which will get him one step closer to loving her instead of me. But I'm not allowed. The universe said so.

"Cleo and Larry, sittin' in a tree, just like dates for the Bling Bling would be." Lisa Lee, walking back to her desk, smirks at her own brilliance.

I glare at her, but my evil eye only hits the back of her head. What she thinks doesn't matter. I've got my offerings for the universe tomorrow, and I'm ready to go.

When Dad picks me up, I rush to the car and scrunch down in my seat. I can't risk Larry running over and telling Dad that he hopes Uncle Arnie likes his monkey. That would take a long time to explain.

"What's wrong?" Dad asks.

"Oh, nothing, just ready to go home!" Luckily, Dad

doesn't ask me anything else; he just shakes his head, mumbling something about kids, and turns up a podcast.

When we're safely out of the parking lot, I sit up straighter. That's when I see something on the dashboard of the car.

A postcard!

I reach out and grab it. "Is this from Uncle Arnie?" I ask. But before Dad can even open his mouth, I have my answer.

SOMEONE IN ALAMOGORDO, NEW MEXICO, LOVES YOU! is what it says on the front. HOME OF THE WORLD'S LARGEST PISTACHIO!

There's also a picture of a person looking very small while standing next to . . . well, I guess it's the world's largest pistachio. Not a real one, though; it's a huge statue, probably thirty feet tall.

"Yeah, I'm not sure what your uncle's up to, but it sure looks like he's having an adventure," Dad says as I turn over the postcard and read.

Cool quote for Cleo: a drop of love, no matter how small, can be detected in river, lake, or endless sea! Live for friendship, love & magic!!!!! From ewe-no-hoooooo!

I figure out Uncle Arnie's code quickly this time. You Know Who.

"Do you have any idea what these postcards are about?" Dad asks.

"No, not really." That's the quickest and easiest answer I have. But inside, I know there's a meaning to each one. Uncle Arnie is trying to tell me something; I just don't know what!

One thing I *do* know is that I am not going to call him again. I learned my lesson. What happened last time, with the Southern lady calling me a ghost child, was just too strange. I can't imagine what's going on in Uncle Arnie's household, and I don't even want to try!

Instead I look at one side of the postcard and then the other, again and again before bedtime. I don't come to any great conclusions while I'm awake, but after I go to sleep and wake up in the morning, there's an idea in my head. I think it came to me in a dream. Like most dreams I have, it didn't make much sense, but I definitely remember a giant pistachio. That's how I know it had something to do with Uncle Arnie's postcard. I've never dreamed of a giant pistachio before . . . and I doubt I ever will again!

In the part I remember, I'm standing by the pistachio in Alamogordo, New Mexico, and though there's not a drop of water in any direction, a red-haired tour guide, maybe Terri, asks if I've been to the lake. Then we're magically transported to a lake surrounded by thick evergreen trees. The guide says it's a shame the lake is so low. "All it needs is rain. Just a few more drops of water and it'll be all right."

Then the really weird part—a lame spaceship, looking like two dinner plates facing each other, lands on the shore of the lake. Its roof opens, and guess whose head pops out? Pandaroo's! The Terri look-alike says goodbye, climbs into the spaceship on a rope ladder, and flies off.

When I open my eyes in the morning, the first thing I do is turn my head and see the love potion bottle across the room from me. It looks more magical than ever as the Saturday sun streams through the window and shines on it.

Drops! Drops of water in a lake. Drops of love potion. Somehow, all the wackiness in my dream has led me to a perfectly sensible idea.

I reread the postcard. **A drop of love, no matter how small, can be detected in river, lake, or endless sea!** A drop of love equals a drop of love *potion.* That's got to be what Uncle Arnie means. What else *could* he mean? I know I promised not to use the potion until I had the instructions, but here they are—finally! They're not exactly clear or understandable, but neither is Uncle Arnie.

I don't need to call him or the strange ladies at his house. I know what to do.

It's time to use the potion.

I unzip my backpack and pull out my offerings for the universe—Larry's monkey; Dad's glasses; and finally, a page from the *Healthyland* play, which I've decided to use as the extension of me and Madison. It was during the play that we became friends; it was the place where we realized that no matter how different we seemed, we had things in common.

I lay these three important items on my dresser—in front of the red bottle. I take a breath and pull off the top. I begin to tip it over and . . .

DING DONG!

Someone's here for the Siren Call.

16

I quickly put the top back on the potion as I hear Dad greeting Madison. By the time I toss the bottle into my backpack, followed by my offerings, Madison's standing at my bedroom door.

"Ready?" she asks.

"Ready!" I smile, but inside I'm a little less than ready. I was just about to use Uncle Arnie's love potion—without the official instructions. Is that really the right thing to do, with only his postcard from Alamogordo and my own silly dream as direction? One minute ago I was ready to tip the bottle's contents all over Larry's monkey, Dad's glasses, and the *Healthyland* page, but now I'm not sure. What should I do?

The doorbell rings again, so I can't answer that question yet.

"Cleo! Are we expecting someone else?" From down the hall, Dad sounds confused.

Oops. I forgot to tell him about Samantha coming over, but I also forgot something else—that it meant he'd be seeing Paige (ugh!). I run out of my bedroom to meet them at the door. I don't want anything happening between Dad and Paige that I'm not there to see.

"Well, this is a nice surprise," Dad says, too happily. "Cleo didn't tell me you two were coming over."

"Some things never change," Paige replies, and they both chuckle. It's a chuckle I don't like. I don't want them chuckling. Why couldn't Paige leave Samantha at the curb and let her come to the door by herself? We're not children anymore!

Sam knows the way to my room, so she walks past the adults with a quick "Bye, Mom" and zips down the hall. I don't leave the doorway. I need to keep watching.

"Do you want to come in for a few minutes? Have some tea or coffee?" Dad asks.

Paige has got to say no to this dumb invitation! She's all dressed up in a tight skirt and blouse; she must have things to do. Plus, who says yes to tea or coffee when it's eighty degrees outside? I turn and start off toward my room, but I stop when I hear what Paige says next.

"That'd be nice, Bradley. Do you have any caffeine-free tea?"

No, no, no, no, no, I think. *We only have tea that will keep you up all night. We have extra-amped-up caffeinated tea; it will make you bounce off the walls and the ceiling!*

"Sure, come on in," Dad says, and Paige strolls toward our kitchen, her high heels click-click-clicking on our hardwood floors.

Ugh. There's nothing I can do about it . . . until we get to the lake and do the *LLAMADA DE LA SIRENA*. This means I have to leave them alone, whether I like it or not.

I run to my room, where Madison is sitting on my bed, petting Toby. Toby likes her so much that he didn't even run and bark when Samantha and her mom rang our doorbell. He's going to miss Madison when she goes away after the Bling Bling Summer Fling. Three months is a long time. And to a dog, it'll feel like twenty-one months! Or it could be forever, if Madison chooses Lisa Lee and Kylie Mae over me.

Samantha's on the other side of the room, letting Millie the millipede crawl on her hand. I have the feeling she and Madison are both nervous; that's why they're playing with my animals instead of talking to each other.

"Sam, are you going to wish for your mom and my dad to be together?" I ask loudly, without even saying hi.

Sam jumps a little. "I'm not allowed to tell!" she says, but her face looks truly confused, like she hadn't even considered the idea. Then she adds, "I thought he liked Terri."

"He did. I mean, he does. He still does," I say. "Okay. Just wanted to make sure. So, your charm is going to be for yourself?"

Madison looks at me like I should know better. "We're not supposed to tell, Cleo. It says so in the book."

"Sorry," I say to both of them, though I'm sick of testing my patience and would really, really like to know what both of them are wishing for! "I'm nervous, I guess."

"We all are," Madison says, mature person that she is. "So, are we going to sit around here or are we going to do it?"

Of course. It's time to do the Siren Call.

We sling our backpacks over our shoulders and make our way toward the front door. Dad and Paige are at the kitchen table with mugs in front of them. They're not sitting too close together, thank goodness, and it doesn't look like we've interrupted anything romantic. It barely looks like they were talking.

They just don't look right together. They never did. They don't look like Terri and Dad used to. After we do the *LLAMADA DE LA SIRENA,* Terri will be the one drinking decaffeinated tea here with Dad, like it should be.

"Have fun, girls," Paige says. We all nod without much of a response.

"Call and check in if you're gone longer than an hour," Dad says. I shout for Toby, but Dad says we don't need to take him, since he wants to jog around the lake later anyway.

"Oh, you jog?" asks Paige. Maybe I'm imagining it, but she sounds like she's impressed, like the next thing she's going to do is squeeze his biceps and tell him what nice muscles he has. She'd better not! He has no muscles at all!

I take Madison and Sam across the street. We walk on the dirt path until we reach the meadow that leads all the way to the bank of the lake. It's warm out and the sun is shining, so people are all over the place. A large group of ladies is taking a yoga class, while families and friends are having picnics. Even the people who are by themselves, reading books or snoozing, look like they're having a good time. All of them are too busy to care about three girls by the edge of the lake.

We sit on the ground and open our backpacks. Madison pulls out a ziplock bag filled with shells she took from the vase in her house's entryway. I start looking through them right away. I don't know if it's true, but I like to think that shells are like snowflakes and fingerprints, with no two being alike. How could they be? The water and sand and air affect each one a little bit differently, so some look chipped and some look perfect—just like people. "Why'd you bring so many?" I ask.

"Well, if we need to make holes in them to put them on the string, I figured some of them might break."

"Good thinking," Sam says. "Let me get my things. . . ." Her voice trails off as she digs in her backpack. Then she pops up holding two items for making holes in shells—a small pair of sharp scissors and something that looks like a teeny, tiny screwdriver.

My only item to bring was the string. That was easy because my dad has junk drawers filled with old computer cords, rolls of tape, random stamps, and other things he'll never miss. I throw the wad of string on the grass between us. Madison and Sam look at me like I just barfed up a big hair ball.

"What?" I ask.

"I thought—" Madison starts.

"I expected a *ball* of string," Sam says over her. "Not a tangled-up mess."

"You expect my house to have a nice, neat ball of string?"

Madison and Sam laugh; they've both been there enough to understand. But now that we've contributed our items, it's time to get started. One by one, we each manage to pull out strings long enough to make necklaces; then we pick shells and poke holes in them. Madison was right; a few of them crack and break. I'm making three necklaces, so I have to slow down and be more careful. Eventually I get the hang of it. Then I remember that I want the necklaces to fall off soon, so I take Sam's scissors and scrape the sharp blade against the edges of my strings to fray them a little.

"Ooh, good idea!" Sam says. It feels nice, getting a compliment from her after all this time. "Let me have the scissors when you're done."

Once she and Madison have thinned out their necklace strings too, we walk to the edge of the water to dip our shells in. That part is easy, except for the tips of my sneakers getting wet. It's the part that comes next—deciding what to sing—that isn't easy at all. Of course it'll be a Ryder

Landry love song, but which one? Sam suggests "Love Monsoon" (*"Love is a monsoon, a typhoon, it takes you over and spins you around!"*), but Madison doesn't think we should sing that next to a body of water, and I have to agree. Madison votes for "You and Me on a Boat in the Sea," another water-themed love song. I love that one too, but when I make my suggestion, Madison and Sam both realize there is no other choice.

"Only One."

What else could it be?

We sing it happily to the world. We're Landers and we want everyone to know. *"You don't want just anyone, you only want your only one . . ."*

Sam raises her arms into the air and sings louder, so we do it too. *"The one who always stuns, the one who never runs, the one who's there for fun . . ."*

We might not have the best pitch, but we're making it up with power. It's a beautiful day, the LA air is semi-fresh, and for this little moment, life is almost as awesome as a Ryder Landry love song. We finish loud and proud: *"The one who will be by your side forever, the one who will turn on you never, never ever, she's your Onnnnnly Onnnnnne!"*

When we turn away from the lake, the ladies from the yoga class are staring at us. "Namaste!" Sam shouts to them. We learned that word in Janet the Recreational Wellness teacher's Spiritual Growth class, where we do things like yoga and drumming and meditation—the stuff my dad calls "New Age mumbo jumbo." Madison and I put our hands in a prayer position in front of our hearts and shout "Namaste" too. The ladies should know this word, but they just look at us strangely, then go back to their downward facing dog yoga pose.

Madison, Sam, and I take turns helping each other put on our necklaces. Samantha ties mine too tight at first, but she loosens it when I let out a little "ow." We all agree that the string is slightly scratchy, but as necklaces, they actually look pretty good. I'm sure Ryder would like them too; according to *Zip! Pow!* magazine, he likes a girl who "revels in her uniqueness."

With our song sung and our necklaces on, it's time for our offerings. We settle back down on the ground and go through our backpacks. One by one, I pull out my items: Dad's glasses, the page from *Healthyland,* and Larry's monkey.

But there's one more thing in my backpack the other girls don't know about. The love potion.

My hand wraps around the edges of the glass bottle, edges that are sharp and smooth at the same time.

Should I use it?

And if I don't use it now, when will I?

Trying not to be too obvious, I turn my back, just a little, from Madison and Samantha. With my hand still in my backpack, I pull the top off the bottle. There's a small

POP, but to me it sounds like an explosion. I glance behind me, but they haven't heard the noise.

I take a peek at what Sam has brought out, hoping it might help me figure out her wish. But her offering must be microscopic, because it's wrapped in what looks like one square of toilet paper. Unless the one square of toilet paper *is* her offering. Ewww, if Larry used that to wipe his butt, that would be the grossest thing ever!

I sneak a glance at Madison's offering too. It's something I've seen in her room every time I've been there, hanging off the edge of the bulletin board above her desk. It's a laminated photo hanging on a long string—the VIP badge from the Ryder concert she went to with Lisa Lee and Kylie Mae! Of all the things Madison owns—and she owns a *lot* of things—that is one of her favorite, most treasured possessions.

Madison has never talked about liking any boy other than Ryder Landry. Could she be using the Siren Call to bring Ryder Landry to her? It seems far-fetched, considering he's a big star traveling the world, but I've seen plenty of strange and magical things happen since I've moved to California, and I *have* to think anything is possible. Otherwise I wouldn't be here right now, about to call the universe for three different wishes.

It's time.

I'm still not sure I'm doing the right thing, but I do it

anyway. Hunching over my backpack, I sneak out the love potion, and carefully—very carefully—tip it over so a nice blob plops onto Dad's broken glasses. It feels smooth and soft as I smear it onto one of the lenses. The next drop falls on the piece of paper with the words of the play on it. I fold up the paper so the potion can't escape. Finally, I pick up Larry's monkey and turn it over. His two little feet are flat on the bottom. I tip the bottle one last time, but before a drop comes out, Madison's voice shocks me.

"What are you doing?"

I turn my head, but Madison and Sam aren't behind me anymore. They're standing, looking down at me—and everything I've done.

"I'm . . ." I try to speak. "I'm . . ."

"She's using the love potion!" Madison announces to Samantha.

"That's the potion?" Sam asks, kneeling down by me. "Can I see?"

"I—I don't know," I stammer. I don't want to give her the potion, but I can't figure out how to say no either.

"You mean you weren't going to share it?" Madison asks. She sounds like she's accusing me of some kind of crime, and I suddenly realize I'm a terrible, terrible person. How could I *not* share it? What kind of friend would that make me?

"No, no, I was going to share it. I was just putting it on my stuff first." That sounds selfish and greedy, but it's not as bad as not sharing the potion at all. I hand the bottle to Madison.

"Well, good!" she says, flashing a satisfied smile. "Did your uncle finally send the instructions?"

"Not . . . exactly," I answer. "But close enough. He sent a postcard and it sounds like it's safe to use a drop."

"Great!" says Madison, turning over the bottle and pouring much more than a drop on her Ryder Landry VIP badge. I grit my teeth, worried about how much she's using, as she rubs it all over like she's giving Ryder a face massage.

"My turn!" says Sam. Madison hands her the bottle and she holds it up to the sun, turning it around in her hand, looking at it from every angle. "Cool!" she says, sprinkling way too many drops of potion onto her folded-up piece of toilet paper.

Sam hands it back to me. The liquid barely fills the bottom of the bottle now. But both she and Madison look so happy and optimistic, I know I made the right choice in sharing the potion. Not that it was actually a *choice,* of course.

I give Madison and Samantha a weak smile and turn my back slightly again, putting a small drop on Mono's feet. I let out a sigh, relieved that this is almost over, but that feeling doesn't last for long.

"Is that Larry's monkey?" Sam asks.

I quickly hide it behind my back.

"It's still there, Cleo," says Madison. She's right. Just because Sam can't see the monkey right now doesn't mean she didn't see it at all.

"Are you asking the universe for Larry?" Sam asks. "You said you didn't like him." To me it sounds like an accusation.

"I . . . don't," I sputter. "I'd tell you everything if I could, but I can't. The spell says so."

Samantha looks more disappointed than angry. "He always has that monkey, every day," she says.

"Well, if the monkey's that special, maybe it'll get the universe's attention," I say. "I want it to listen."

"Yeah, me too," Samantha says. Then she mutters "wow" and walks to the edge of the water.

Madison looks at me, then at Sam. She understands why I have Larry's monkey, and I hope she's not judging me like Sam seems to be. "Cleo's got a lot of complicated wishes going on," Madison tells Sam. "And someday, this is all going to make sense." We join Sam at the edge of the water.

"I get it," Sam says, though she doesn't sound totally convinced. "So are we going to do this?"

We do it. First I chuck Dad's glasses far and they make a decent little splash. Madison's badge follows. Samantha's toilet paper doesn't go far; it flutters quietly onto the water's surface, and if any item fell out of it, I couldn't see. I fling the folded *Healthyland* page like a Frisbee. The paper goes pretty far, but the splash isn't impressive.

The only thing left is the monkey. I feel the cool wood against my hand, the carved fur against my fingers.

Madison and Samantha stare at me, waiting.

I look at the monkey's cute pink face, smiling at me with its mischievous eyes.

Larry's had this with him every day since spring break. It's much more important than Dad's old glasses . . . or Samantha's toilet paper (whatever that was!) . . . even Madison's Ryder Landry badge. What would I tell Larry at school on Monday? That I lost it?

I could never do that. Not to a friend.

I look at Madison and Sam. I shake my head.

As I'm bending down to put the monkey back in my backpack and the girls are telling me I'm doing the right thing, a loud, gruff voice interrupts us. "What are you kids doing?" All three of us turn around.

Red Shorts!

"I will call the authorities!" he shouts. He's not coming toward us, though; he's staying on the dirt path and walking in place. But he's stretching his neck to look past us.

"You're littering?" he yells. "Why in the world would you come to this beautiful lake to destroy it?"

While I hardly feel like tossing a few small items into the lake is going to destroy it, I also don't want to argue with him—especially when he's attempting to unzip the little pack on his butt while walking in place. Maybe he's reaching for his phone! Luckily, it's a tough task and takes him a while, so I do what any smart, focused Focus! student would do: assess the situation, determine my options, and finally shout, "Run!"

We scramble as quickly as we can, bumping into each other as we throw all our supplies in the closest backpacks and run off with them unzipped.

"I'm gonna keep an eye out for you kids!" Red Shorts shouts. He's still walking in place, holding his phone in his fist and shaking it at us.

"Please don't call anyone!" Sam yells, running. "We're innocent little children!"

"It's not littering! It's love!" I shout.

I didn't think our short legs could outrun the walking man, but when we turn around a minute later, breathing heavily, we see his red shorts walking in the other direction. We all break out laughing, and I'm glad Samantha has forgotten about Larry's monkey, at least for the moment.

"Did he give up?" Madison wonders.

"I don't know," I say, "but I think we'd better get back to my house fast!"

As we walk back, I can't talk. My heart is pounding from running. I'm smiling because of Red Shorts. And though I'm a little upset about how Sam reacted to the monkey, I'm excited about all the great things that are going to happen next.

I hope.

17

That night at bedtime, I get into my pj's without even being asked, and go to say good night to Dad, who's reading in the living room. This reminds me that it's been a long time since I opened *Quantum Physics, Biocentrism, and the Universe as We Know It* . . . but right now, I have more important things to think about. Like the necklace I'm holding for Dad behind my back.

He smiles and puts his book down. "Did you have a good day with your friends?"

I tell him I did and thank him for letting them come over. I could ask him if he had a good day with Paige, but I don't really want to know the answer. At least she was gone by the time we got back to the house. "I'm going to bed," I tell him. "But I wanted to give you something first."

"Something good?" he asks.

"Only if you think something your most darling daughter made for you is something good."

"In that case, yes!" Dad pats the spot next to him on the couch, so I sit down. "What is it?"

I tell him to close his eyes and he does. When I tell him to open them, my hands are dangling the necklace in front of him.

His expression is blank for a second; then he smiles. "A shell!" he says. I can't tell if the enthusiasm is real or not. He takes it from me and looks at it more carefully. "That's a nice one."

"It's not just a shell," I tell him. "It's a necklace. See, I've got one too!" I pull mine out from underneath my pajama shirt and show him.

He smiles, but he's touching the string, which, as I know already, is going to be scratchy against his neck. "Hmmm," he finally says. "I never thought of myself as a necklace kind of guy."

"That's why I thought it'd be great. New glasses, new necklace. Let me put it on you!" Without waiting for him to say yes, I stand up on the couch, push him forward, and point his head down so I can tie the string at the back of his neck.

"Give me a little more space," he says, bringing his hand to his neck.

Jeez, adults and their "space." But there's a slight cough in Dad's voice, so I loosen it a little and tie a knot, noticing the parts where I thinned out the string with the scissors. This necklace won't last long. Good.

I step away and sit back down on the couch. Dad arranges the shell against his neck. "How does it look?"

"Great!" I say, though maybe I'm exaggerating. I could picture this necklace on a dad who has shaggy blond hair and lives on the beach and drives a convertible, but my dad wears glasses and sits at a computer and drinks iced Americanos at a coffeehouse. It doesn't look bad; it just doesn't look like him.

"Let me see." Dad gets up and walks to the bathroom, with me right behind him. He looks in the mirror and smiles. "I like it," he says, and this time I believe him. "You know, your mom collected shells like this."

"Really?" I don't remember any shells in Ohio. "Did they have them at the lake where you met?"

"No, not there. But her parents were from the East Coast, and whenever she went to the beach in New Jersey, she'd pick a favorite shell and save it. I wish I knew where they were now. You could make more necklaces with them." He touches the shell on his neck and looks at it closely in the mirror. "Yep, she would've loved this one."

I'm not sad, but what Dad is saying almost makes me feel like I am. So I change my attitude. I have to keep my final goal in mind. "Does Terri love shells too?" I ask.

Dad turns away from the mirror and looks at me. "I'm not sure. She likes the beach, though, remember?"

"Yeah. Maybe we can all go to the beach again some-time." Worried I might sound too eager, I add, "You know, as friends."

Dad sighs. "Maybe. We'll see. Now, come on, it's late."

"I know, I know," I say, sighing like he did. "Bedtime."

Dad thanks me again, and I head to my room without complaining. I go to sleep with a smile. The shell reminds him of someone he loved. So we're moving in the right direction.

Now the necklace just needs to fall off.

On Monday morning, my necklace is still in place. It was hard to sleep with it on, and when I finally drag myself out of bed, I look in the mirror and see a thin red line around my neck—a scratchy-looking rash from the string.

Yesterday the necklace made me feel like a unique girl Ryder Landry could love, but today I realize it could be something for people like Lisa Lee and Kylie Mae to make fun of. So I put on a T-shirt with a high-enough collar that the necklace is mostly hidden below.

At breakfast I see a red line around Dad's neck too, but he's being a good dad and not complaining. Oh well, if I'm lucky, the universe will spring into action soon and Dad won't be wearing that necklace anymore—and neither will I.

"Cool necklace!" is the first thing I hear when I walk into Kevin's classroom, and to my shock, the words are coming from Lisa Lee!

The strange thing is that she's not saying it in a mean, sarcastic way. I put my hand to my neck, and sure enough, my necklace has popped out of my T-shirt a little. Maybe my life is changing already.

Then I see that she's talking to Madison, not me. Of course. I shove the shell back under my T-shirt and take my seat.

"Oh, thanks. I made it over the weekend." Madison lightly touches the string around her neck. If she's got a rash, I can't see it from my chair.

"Wow, if you made more, I bet you could sell them. They're so, like, back to nature; stores in Beverly Hills would pay a *ton* for them. You'd be an awesome jewelry designer!"

"Yeah," echoes Kylie Mae.

Come on! If Lisa Lee had seen the necklace on me first, it'd be dorky and loserish. But because it's on Madison, it's cool.

Sixth grade is so unfair.

For the first time in days, I don't avoid Larry at lunch. He's already sitting by himself when I get to the lunchroom with the turkey, lettuce, and butter sandwich my dad packed. I plop myself down, and he looks at me with eyes that are so happy, I feel terrible—for avoiding him, for lying so he'd give me his Costa Rican treasure, and most of all, for almost throwing Mono in the lake! But what other choice did I have when he decided to declare his love for me? It'd be way too embarrassing and uncomfortable to talk to him about how I really feel.

"Hey," I say, unzipping my backpack.

"Hey," he says back. "I thought maybe we weren't eating lunch together anymore." The way he says it makes me want to cry. Thank goodness I don't have to tell him that I "lost" his monkey.

"Nah, I've just had a lot of things to do, a lot of things on my mind," I say. "But today I have a little friend who wants to say hello to you!" I pull out the monkey and, with a flourish, place him on the table. "Ta-da!"

Larry gets a big smile on his face. "Oh, great, thanks! Did your uncle like him?"

"Huh?" I ask.

"Your uncle."

"What?"

"The one going to Costa Rica."

Oh, right! I was so proud of myself for doing the right thing and returning the monkey, I forgot exactly what I said to take him away in the first place. "Right, yeah," I reply. "He said he can't wait to see monkeys in the wild.

And if he sees one like this at a gift shop or the airport, he'll buy me one."

"He doesn't have to do that," Larry says. "You could have mine."

His? This cute little monkey sitting right in front of us? The monkey that has been by his side for weeks and has only been away from him for the two days I took him home? If that's not a sign of love, I don't know what is! Maybe I *should* have thrown it in the lake. . . .

"No, no, no," I say. "You told me how important he is to you."

With his mouth full of sloppy joe, Larry nods for a moment. Then, after a swallow, he says, "He is. But my mom was really proud of me for giving him up for the weekend. And I didn't feel too nervous or jumpy or anything without him. That's what I was afraid of. I could fall asleep and everything."

So Larry, without his monkey, slept better this weekend than I did with this shell necklace around my neck!

"Plus, if you have him," Larry continues, "I'll always know where he is!"

"No, I can't," I say. "I shouldn't." I'm squirming like my whole body is covered with scratchy necklaces, feeling like I shouldn't have sat down here. Larry's offer is way too meaningful, and it comes with a lot of responsibility— responsibility I don't want.

"Hey, anybody sitting here?"

185

Oh boy, it's Samantha. If she wanted to, she could tell Larry what I did—or almost did—with Mono. My whole body tenses up . . . waiting.

"Nice necklace," Larry says as Sam takes the seat across from him.

"Thanks," Samantha says, taking a bite of her sloppy joe. With serious eyes, she looks at me. Can she see in my eyes how much I'm hoping that she doesn't say anything?

Maybe she does, because she smiles toward Larry and says, "Hey, your monkey's back!" Then she looks at me and raises her eyebrows knowingly. Sam's not going to bust me. My muscles unsqueeze.

"Yeah, but I've decided I don't need him so much anymore," Larry tells her. "You want him?"

Sam doesn't think it over for a second. "Sure!" she says, picking him up. "He's cute!"

Well, that's not what I expected. Why isn't Larry begging me, his one true love, to be the keeper of his special memento? Doesn't he want us linked for the rest of our lives, now and forever? Instead, Sam is now making Mono bounce along the table as she makes "ooh ooh ahh ahh" monkey noises!

Madison has also gotten a sloppy joe today, and I see her walking toward us from the lunch line. As she gets closer I say, "Hey" . . . but she doesn't slow down.

In a low voice, almost a whisper, she says, "I'm . . .

uh . . . going to . . ." She nods her head toward the other side of the lunchroom—and keeps walking. When I look in the direction she nodded, I see the opposite of what I wished for at the lake—she's walking straight over to Lisa Lee and Kylie Mae's table! They greet her with a squeal of excitement while Ronnie and Lonnie Cheseboro grunt and say, "Yo."

"Well, that's not super cool," Sam says.

I don't say anything. My insides have gotten gray and sad and mushy all of a sudden. It's only lunchtime on Monday, and I'm already afraid that all the hard work we put in on our Siren Call—the string, the shells, the offerings, running away from Red Shorts—was a total waste of time.

I don't want to see anyone during outdoor break, so I go to the last place anyone would want to spend a significant amount of time—the girls' bathroom. I sit on the toilet, and despite how terrible I feel, I'm smart enough to put the lid down while I play a Pig Mania game on my phone. No loud noises or other surprises are going to cause me to drop my phone in the toilet. As upset as I am, I still have enough focus to avoid that. If I could ever tell her this story, Roberta would be proud.

I hear voices come and go—some I recognize and some I don't. I hear a bunch of people pee and a couple of people poop, and almost everyone washes their hands. If anyone wants to use my stall, they just pull on the door and give up when they realize someone's inside.

Until Lisa Lee and Kylie Mae make their entrance.

"He wants to kiss," Lisa Lee says with an icked-out tone to her voice, "but I just want him to hang out with me at outdoor break and maybe hold hands. Is Lonnie like that?"

"Yeah," Kylie Mae says.

"He'd better not think I'm going to kiss him at the Bling Bling. He probably thinks I'll be so scared on the rides I'll jump into his arms or something. If that's his plan, he's barking up the wrong girl!"

I laugh on the inside because I think she means "barking up the wrong tree." For that second I'm not concentrating on my video game, and when one of them pulls at the stall door, I'm surprised.

CRASH! My phone drops to the floor.

Dad was smart enough to put a thick plastic case on it, so it doesn't break, but it bounces underneath the door and out into the bathroom. Oh no.

"Hey, I got your phone," Lisa Lee calls, not knowing I'm the one behind the door.

I disguise my voice, making it low and grumbly. "Leave it on the sink; I'm busy."

Lisa Lee and Kylie Mae both laugh. "Who is that? Do we know you?" Lisa Lee asks.

Ugh, I do not want to have this conversation! "No," I say, mumbly and scratchy. "I'm new here."

"Hmmm," says Lisa Lee, who's followed by Kylie Mae with a similar "Hmmm." Lisa Lee picks up where Kylie Mae left off. "That's funny. I haven't heard of any new girls here. Especially none that wear Cleo Nelson's unattractive sneakers."

There's nothing I can do now, so I respond in my own voice. "They're not unattractive—they're unique!" They really are. They're bright pink and I've drawn my animated characters all over them. I may not be proud of many things, but I'm proud of these sneakers. I open the door to find Lisa Lee and Kylie Mae standing side by side.

"Ewww, she didn't flush," says Kylie Mae.

"I was sitting on the lid!"

"Still," says Kylie Mae.

"Are you gonna give me my phone?" I ask. I have visions of them tossing it in the trash can or, even worse, throwing it in the toilet.

"I don't want your dumb phone," Lisa Lee says, handing it back to me. "You probably don't have any good apps or games anyway."

"Thanks," I say, not meaning it. I head toward the door.

"Hey, we're sorry about the Bling Bling Summer Fling," Lisa Lee's voice says behind me.

I turn around. "What about it?"

"She doesn't know," Kylie Mae whispers to Lisa Lee, though I'm standing right there and can hear her.

"Madison's coming with us," Lisa Lee says.

"To the Bling Bling?" I ask.

"Duh," says Kylie Mae, and I don't blame her. Of course that's what she meant.

I try to cover up my surprise and sadness with a forced smile. "That's okay," I say. "I've got other plans anyway." I open the door, thinking that if what Lisa Lee just told me is true, my other plans will be to not go to the Bling Bling at all. I'll stay home and start convincing Dad to move back to Ohio.

As the door closes behind me, I think I hear Kylie Mae say one more thing. "Her necklace isn't as cute as Madison's."

18

When Dad picks me up, his necklace is still tight around his neck. He doesn't complain at all, but I see him scratch at it every once in a while when we're at a stoplight.

"Dad, you can take off that necklace if you want," I tell him.

"No, I like it," he says with a smile that may or may not be real.

"No, you don't. It's stupid. It's ugly. And it's uncomfortable and it's scratching your neck."

"That's not true," he says, then thinks about it. "Well, that's half true. Yes, it is a little uncomfortable and, yes, it's scratching my neck, but it's not ugly. And it's definitely not stupid. Nothing you make for me could ever be stupid."

I don't believe that for a second, but it kind of makes me smile, since it's another one of those types of things parents have to say to their kids. I want to put Dad to the test.

"Okay, what if I made you a smoothie of kale and wasabi and onion and Tabasco and then topped it off with mud?"

Dad looks at me with a grossed-out expression, but he gulps and says, "Delicious."

"Okay, what if I made a sculpture out of Toby's turds, spray-painted it gold, and wrote 'World's Greatest Dad' on it?"

"That would be . . . delightful," Dad forces himself to say.

"Then you are the World's Greatest Dad." I laugh.

"You're right," he says. "But please don't make me that sculpture."

It's nice to laugh for a minute, but inside the house, as I walk from the front door to my room, I make the mistake of glancing toward Dad's office in the dining room. His computer with the biggest screen has a website up, and even from across the house, I can see white bells and ribbons, doves and cakes, and fancy cursive writing that reads "Save the Date: We're Getting Married!"

Whatever smile I might have had on my face is gone now.

On one side of the page, faded in the background, is an old-fashioned photo of a dark-haired four- or five-year-old girl dressed like a bride in a little white dress and veil, her tiny feet in grown-up heels way too big for her. I immediately know that this is a young version of Samantha's mom. The photo probably came from the scrapbook she gave my dad the other day!

There's no picture of a little boy on the other side, but I bet Dad doesn't know where any of his old photos are. He can't keep track of anything in our dumb, messy house. He doesn't even know what happened to my mom's collection of shells from the New Jersey beach.

We're Getting Married?

Suddenly it all makes sense! This is what he and Paige have been talking about all this time! On the phone, at school, over coffee and tea. Now that I think of it, Dad was dressed kind of nicely for the art show, probably because he *knew* he'd see her there! And he *says* he's been taking longer hikes and bike rides . . . but maybe that's not what he's been doing at all. He's been going on dates and not even telling his only daughter!

It seems crazy and out of control and way too fast, but that's the way Dad can be! He moved us to Los Angeles because of Terri, and he didn't tell me about *that* forever. He was *in love* with Terri back then, and I never knew. I just thought she was a girlfriend.

So it's true. He's getting married—to Samantha's mom—and hasn't told me yet. So much for the World's Greatest Dad.

I'm not sure whether I want to throw up or cry or punch things, but whatever I'm doing, it's going to be in my room, far away from Dad.

I stomp to my room, pull *POCIÓNES FANTÁSTICOS* from under my bed, and throw it back to the ground. That book is *estúpido, muy muy estúpido*! I crush it with my foot, not even caring that I have to return it to the library. No one else in the world should ever check out this idiotic book, ever! The Siren Call hasn't solved anything; it's only made everything worse. And I have a red rash around my neck to prove it.

I open up my desk drawers, looking around for a pair of scissors. I finally find some under a bunch of Pandaroo storyboards I never finished. I walk over to my mirror and pull the scratchy string away from my neck. I probably shouldn't be taking a pair of scissors to this important part of my body when I'm this upset and my eyes are teary, but the necklace is strangling me. Dad hates me using the word *hate,* but guess what? I don't care! I hate this necklace! I hate love potions, I hate love charms, and I hate love!

I lift the scissors to the frayed string, but before I make my first snip, I see something behind me, reflected in the mirror. It's small and rectangular and has a colorful photo on the front.

Not another postcard?

I put down the scissors, walk over to Millie's terrarium, and pick it up.

Yep, it's another card from Uncle Arnie. Why is he bothering me again so soon?

At first I liked these cards, as weird and confusing as they were, but today Uncle Arnie is more annoying than anything else.

I look at the stupid card anyway. What else is there to do with it?

I SAW THE METEOR CRATER AND RV PARK IN WINSLOW, ARIZONA! it says across the top. And sure enough, the picture is of a canyon-like hole in the ground with nothing around it in any direction except for dirt, dirt, and more dirt. There's a wooden boardwalk over a small section of the hole, and the people standing on it are teeny-weeny, so this crater must be gigantic.

On the back, Uncle Arnie has written:

What did the asteroid say to the Earth? "Time for a last-ditch effort!" Get it? Because it made a really big ditch! Don't reach for the stars, Cleo; reach for the asteroids!

Yep, once again Uncle Arnie has sent a postcard that barely makes any sense, at a time when I really don't need any more mysteries. But I can't ignore it either. It has to mean something. All the others did.

I can sort of guess what a "last-ditch effort" is, but I look

195

it up online anyway. It says it's a term from when wars were fought in ditches. The last-ditch effort was the last desperate attempt.

I sit on my bed holding the postcard over my crossed legs. So what does Uncle Arnie mean with this one?

I scratch at my necklace.

I pat Toby's furry head when he pokes it on the bed by my knee.

I look at the postcard again. I read the facts on the back in small type. What were the chances of this asteroid hitting our planet fifty thousand years ago and now becoming a tourist attraction where you can take photos, buy souvenirs, and have lunch at Subway? That asteroid was minding its own business, probably having a fine time zooming through the solar system, and BAM! It hit our little planet. And it didn't slam into the other side of the world; it hit the state right next to mine.

If that can happen, *anything* can . . . right?

The Bling Bling Summer Fling is three days away. School ends the day after that.

Is it time for a last-ditch effort?

I think Uncle Arnie would say yes.

Step one of my last-ditch effort is to try one more charm. And since time is running out, I need Samantha's help.

But will she give it to me?

When we went to Madison's and Sam translated the Siren Call, we might have been moving toward becoming friends again. But after she saw Larry's monkey at the lake, I have no idea what direction we're heading. It could be right off a cliff!

It takes all morning to build up my courage, but I pull Sam aside at outdoor break and ask if she'll translate one last charm—hopefully the charm that will fix everything. I don't tell her exactly what's broken, just that nothing is turning out as I'd hoped.

She absentmindedly touches her necklace. It's still around her neck, which means her wish hasn't come true either. She must be ready for a last-ditch effort too, because she says she'll do it. I sneak *POCIÓNES FANTÁSTICOS* from my backpack to hers, and then I wait.

The rest of the school day passes. Dad drives me home. We eat dinner. I stare at my homework. I look at my phone every five seconds. Nothing from Sam.

Did she change her mind? Did her necklace fall off, so she doesn't care about me anymore?

I put on my pajamas, but I know I'll never fall asleep. Then, just as I'm about to turn off my light and try to go to bed, my phone dings.

Too long to text. Check your email.

I turn on my computer. The subject line of her email is *MENSAJE EN BOTELLA.*

En inglés, she has written, it's MESSAGE IN A BOTTLE.

Messages in bottles have been used since time immemorial.

Okay, I don't know what *immemorial* means, but I'm going to guess it means "a super-long time."

These messages began as a way to study the movements of the seas but soon became a romantic notion. A person who would find your message across a great expanse of water would be the person who understands you, who helps you, and who might be your true love.

Or, to quote Ryder Landry, your *Only One*! This charm is sounding good so far.

Write a letter to the person who will understand your dilemma. Tell him or her, or even the universe, who you are and what you are feeling. Share your deepest wishes and desires, no matter how silly or unattainable they seem.

Sam has written her own note here: "Not sure if 'unattainable' is the word. May be 'unfeasible' or 'unreachable' but I think they're all the same thing."

If Samantha thinks so, I'll believe her. I've got a spell to read!

Decorate a bottle with the colors and designs that mean much to you and deposit the letter inside. When your loving feelings have charged the bottle with positive energy and happy emotions, walk to the edge of a body of water, toss in the bottle, and ask the powers of the universe to listen to your message.

I read the charm again, and then one more time. During my third reading, there's a knock at my door and I nearly jump out of my chair. "What, Dad?" I shout as he opens the door and sticks his head in.

"Sorry, didn't mean to scare you. Five minutes, then lights out."

My mind is full of ideas from reading the instructions, so I don't say anything back.

"Did you hear me?" Dad asks, and I jump again.

"Yeah, yeah. Five minutes."

"I hope it's homework that's captured your attention like that," he says.

I'm barely listening, so I just say, "Yeah, yeah" again.

Five minutes isn't enough time to do everything I need to do, so I say good night to Dad and turn off my light like a good little daughter. I lie in my bed looking at the ceiling (I might as well be in one of those pitch-black restaurants, since I can't see a thing) and wait.

I hear muffled voices coming from the living room. Dad's streaming something on our big screen. I hope it's a short TV show, not a long movie.

I wait.

Finally the voices click off. The house is quiet except for the sound of Dad's socks on the floor and him mumbling to Toby.

I wait more. Teeth are brushed. Water is sloshed around in mouth. Toothpaste is spit. There might be a fart. Or the creaking of a door, I'm not sure.

I wait. I hear a click; that must be Dad's light going off. A door closes. Dad's bed slightly squeaks.

Finally!

I throw off my covers and go over to my computer, turning the volume down so Dad won't hear it start up.

I'm not much of a writer, and I'm definitely not a typist, but I have a lot to say and I can't waste any time judging myself. I need to write what's in my heart.

Dear Ryder,
   Hi! How are you? I know you get a lot of letters and I doubt you'll get this one, since I'm throwing it in a lake, but I could use your help. My name is Cleo Nelson. I'm almost twelve and I live in

Los Angeles, but not in a big mansion like you. I live with my dog, Toby, and Millie, my millipede, and my dad. My dad's okay but he misses his girlfriend, Terri. He thinks he wants to marry someone else, but I know he doesn't.

I like your music because it makes me think about love, and he loved Terri a lot—and my mom too, but she died when I was little. I hope that doesn't bum you out, because we're happy people most of the time and I bet you'd like us.

Just so you know, this is not a love letter—it's a letter about friendship. You helped bring me and my friend Madison closer together, and I'm hoping you can do that again. Maybe you could send her an autographed picture. Or a text. Even if she never knew it came from me, even if it didn't make her choose me over her other friends, I would still be happy because you made her happy. But maybe your pure Landryness will show her other friends that we're not that different. Like you say in your song "Under the Sun": "No matter where you're from, how far you can run, whose heart you have won ... we're all one, under the sun!"

If you don't have time for any of this, I understand and will still be a big fan. Have a good time in Asia!

Your friend, Cleo Nelson

I look at my computer screen and smile. It's done. It's good. Then I notice the clock in the corner. Oh my gosh, it's two in the morning!

I can't print the letter now; my printer makes a really loud GEEEZZZHHH GEEEZZZHHHH noise and would probably wake up Dad. What I *can* do now is copy the letter and send it to Ryder on his website. I once read on the *WickedHappyTeenTime* blog that Ryder can get up to a thousand letters a day, so I know the chances of him reading mine by the end of the school year, three days from now, are about as good as the chances of a giant pistachio growing on a bay tree on the moon.

But I had to try.

My eyes are getting heavy, but I have to stay awake. There's still a lot to do. My plan is to get up super early in the morning while Dad's still asleep, sneak across the street, and toss the letter in the lake before the sun is even up.

But first I need a bottle.

I pull at my door, cringing when it creaks, and open it only enough for me to squeeze through sideways. I tiptoe to the recycling bin in the kitchen and dig around. The cans and glass and plastic all clank against each other noisily. I "shhh" them (why, I'm not sure) and finally find a wine bottle.

I wash it out thoroughly in the kitchen sink, because one thing I've read on the *Hot Cool Fab Teen* website is that Ryder Landry "simply cannot abide alcohol. He doesn't understand why people, especially young people, need it to have fun." He and I agree on that! When I turn off the water, I accidentally hit the garbage disposal. It's as loud as a garbage truck on top of a steam train, but my reflexes are fast and I turn it off in less than one second. I'm feeling pretty proud of myself, when . . .

CRASH! CLANG! I drop the bottle in the sink. It didn't have far to fall, so it doesn't break. Whew! I scoop it up in my hand and stand super still. From far away, Toby lets out one bark. I think Dad mumbles, "Quiet, Toby." It's a sound-asleep type of voice, so I hope I'm safe. I wait one more minute, then turn off the light and sneak back to my room.

My clock says 2:14 a.m. I want to get up at six. Less than four hours of sleep, and there's still more to do. *Last-ditch effort,* I tell myself. *Last-ditch effort.* After this, life goes back to normal. Whatever normal is going to be. Hopefully it means Dad won't be marrying Paige, Larry won't be in love with me, and Madison will be my friend again.

Before all that can happen, I have to decorate the bottle. I open my closet and grab art supplies, barely looking at them. Construction paper, Magic Markers, glitter, glue, ribbons, pipe cleaners, anything. I lie on the floor on my stomach, cutting out photos of Ryder from magazines and pasting some of them to the outside of the bottle. Then I make red and purple hearts out of construction paper and write our names on them—me and Ryder and Madison,

Sam and Larry, Dad and Terri. I paste some of them on the outside and roll some up and put them inside. I find a red ribbon and tie a bow around the top.

The final decoration—the icing on the cake, the roses on the icing—will be some swirls of glitter between the photos, the hearts, and the ribbon. It's going to look magnif . . .

19

"**C**leo! Breakfast!"

My eyes open. The first thing I see is the wood of my bedroom floor. Why? Because my head is on the floor. My body is on the floor. I fell asleep on the floor! A small pool of glue is also on the floor, and my almost completely decorated wine bottle is less than a foot away. I jump to my feet, pick it up, and quickly but gently place it in the bottom drawer of my desk. So much for doing the *MENSAJE EN BOTELLA* before school.

I throw off my pajamas and find some clothes to wear.

"I'm making smoothies!" Dad shouts from the kitchen.

"Great!" I yell back, though I really don't care. He's probably getting all healthy for his wedding to Paige. Since I happen to be around, I get a smoothie too.

I grab my brush and look in the mirror. That's when I see that there is glitter—along with tiny specks of dust and dirt—all over my cheek and the side of my face that was on the floor. I wipe my cheek with my hand . . . or at least I try to. The glitter is not moving. It's glued to my face.

I run to the bathroom. I need to wash my face—bad! I rub soap in my hands and scrub the right side of my face, hard. The dirt kind of comes off, but the glitter does not. I pick up a washcloth and try harder. Still nothing.

I've got two other ideas, but they're dangerously close to where Dad is. Covering the side of my face with one hand, I run to the kitchen sink and grab a sponge and the scrubby thing we use to wash the dishes. Dad, who's working on a smoothie, turns around. "What are you doing?" he asks over the grinding of the blender, but I run back to the bathroom without answering. The rough side of the sponge gets a little of the glitter off, and the scrubby does the rest.

I look in the mirror and sigh with relief. I'm glitter- and dirt-free. Only now the right side of my face is as red as a strawberry smoothie and the other side is normal. For a second I consider taking the sponge and scrubby to the left side of my face so they'll match, but Dad calls me again for breakfast.

He doesn't even bother asking what's up. Dad's seen enough strange stuff around this house; he's starting to know better than to ask.

Even without doing my *MENSAJE EN BOTELLA* this morning, maybe the universe is looking out for me, because (1) my cheek has turned from bright red to a less noticeable pink, and (2) when Dad drops me at school, Paige is *not* in the parking lot. If I saw her and Dad together right now, I just might barf all over both of them.

I even get the chance to express my thankfulness for these small blessings, because today in Recreational Wellness, Janet has decided it's time for a Spiritual Growth class. We're sitting in the gym on individual yoga mats with our legs crossed, waiting to see what "mumbo jumbo" she has in store today. In a voice that works a lot better for activities like crab soccer and kickball, she announces/shouts that "TODAY IS ABOUT GRATITUDE AND BEATITUDE!"

"What do those mean?" Kylie Mae whispers to Lisa Lee behind me.

"Gratitude is being grateful," she whispers back.

"So does *beatitude* mean being beautiful?"

"It better not, because Cleo would be in trouble! Did you see her tomato face?"

"I saw half of it," Kylie Mae replies.

So much for my gratitude! My face barely looked pink in Dad's rearview mirror! I turn around and hiss at them to be quiet—and that is, of course, what Janet hears.

"Cleo! We're meditating today. It's time for clearing the mind, for silence."

I nod, working hard not to roll my eyes. I think Janet is kind of nutty to expect twenty or more sixth graders to sit quietly, unmoving, just breathing, for fifteen minutes, but she tries, yelling as always. "BREATHE IN! BREATHE

OUT! LIVE IN THE MOMENT! DON'T LET YOUR MIND WANDER!"

I try not to let the usual truckload of thoughts barrel through my brain. As I breathe in and out, I try to only think of the things I want from the universe. My friendship with Madison. Dad and Terri. Larry and Samantha. But my mind wanders. Is my face less red now? What's for lunch? Dad gave me money for lunch today. . . .

"BREATHE IN, BREATHE OUT!" shouts Janet in an anything-but-calming manner.

I force my mind to go back to what's important. My friendship with Madison. Dad and Terri. Larry and Samantha. Shepherd's pie! That's what's for lunch!

I mean, my friendship with Madison. Dad and Terri. Larry and Samantha. Breathing in, breathing out.

A heavenly little bell rings, which means our fifteen minutes is over. I can't believe it. I actually feel pretty relaxed.

That feeling doesn't last long, though, because in the gym doorway, I almost bump into Madison. Since she had lunch with Lisa Lee and Kylie Mae the other day—and especially after what they told me in the bathroom—I don't know how to talk to her anymore; I don't know what to say.

I think for a second and come up with something. That something is "Hey." I really am a poet when it comes to choosing the right words.

"Hey," she says back. "I almost fell asleep just now."

I smile. "Yeah, I feel very relaxed."

"See you in the lunchroom," she says, and walks ahead.

Does "See you in the lunchroom" mean she's sitting with me today?

I can't know until I get there. Until then, I have to "live in the moment" . . . but all I can think about is five minutes in the future. Lunch. Lunch. Lunch.

I dawdle before getting in the lunch line, hoping Madison will come by and we can go through it together, but I can smell the brown meat and gravy mingling with the white mashed potatoes and gravy, and I can't wait any longer! I get my food and join Larry and Samantha, who are already sitting together. Sam is waving Larry's (former) monkey around as Larry tries to grab him out of her hand. I might be annoyed if someone was waving around a precious item of mine like this, but Larry's just laughing.

Samantha taps me on the shoulder. "Hate to mention this, Cleo, but you're gonna see it sooner or later." She points over at the popular table. Madison is settling in there again, only this time she's wearing a Ryder Landry T-shirt that must have been under the sweater she had on in Spiritual Growth class.

Even worse, Lisa Lee and Kylie Mae are wearing the same shirts. I recognize the picture of Ryder on them. It's the same photo from the laminated badge Madison threw in the lake. They must have bought the shirts together at the concert.

Does this mean Madison asked the universe to be friends with Lisa Lee and Kylie Mae again? Why would she have asked for that? She could have had that anytime, without doing a charm. I didn't notice in Spiritual Growth whether or not she still had her necklace on. I squint my eyes against the sun streaming in the lunchroom window and try to focus on Madison's neck.

The necklace sure looks like it's still there.

So what's going on?

My original idea must have been right. Madison used her Siren Call to call Ryder Landry. And later today, I'll give him an extra push.

The whole thing has made me lose my appetite, though. I look down at my shepherd's pie, breathe in the yummy aroma, and decide I'll eat it anyway. No point in letting delicious food go to waste, no matter how bummed out I am that the universe hasn't listened to me yet.

When I get home, I grab the decorated wine bottle out of my desk drawer. Even though I fell asleep while making it (and there's still glue and glitter and little pieces of construction paper on my floor to prove it), it doesn't look half bad. I straighten the ribbon I tied at the top and reglue a few of the purple and red hearts on it. My printer wheezes GEEEZZZHHH GEEEZZZHHHH as it prints out the letter I wrote last night and spits it into the tray underneath. I reread it.

I'm not usually the bragging type, but I have to say, it's pretty good. If Ryder happens to pick it randomly from the thousand emails he gets today on his website, he might actually pay attention. And if the letter somehow contacts the universe, *it* might pay attention too. Proud of myself, I roll it tightly and put it in the bottle.

There's one last thing to do. I walk over to my dresser and look at my love potion. At the bottom of the red bottle, there's a super-thin line—almost undetectable.

After all the potion we used during our Siren Call, there's only one drop left.

It's almost gone.

But so what? What more do I have to lose? Time for a last-ditch effort, like the postcard said.

Only this one really will be the *last.*

I take out the stopper and raise the lip of the potion bottle up to the top of the wine bottle. There's so little liquid left, it doesn't even PLOP like it did before; it just quietly slips from one bottle to the other. And it's gone. Done. Over.

If the love potion was ever going to work, it's got to work now.

I put the wine bottle in my backpack and zip it up. I

shout for Dad, telling him I want to get some fresh air and take a walk. "Are you taking Toby?" he asks.

"I guess," I say. When I walk toward the front door to grab Toby's leash, I see Dad at his computers in the dining room. The wedding website is up on the big screen, and he's changing the size of the "Save the Date" font. When Dad realizes where I am, he clicks a button and the screen goes dark.

That jerk! He doesn't want me to see it! His own daughter! The one person closest to him in the whole entire world! Maybe he wants this big wedding announcement to be a beautiful surprise. While Madison and Lisa Lee and Kylie Mae are all doing the hula on the soft sand and surfing the warm waters of Hawaii, Samantha and I will be planning her mom's bridal shower and getting fitted for ugly, irritating bridesmaid dresses. I don't want to wear flowers and ribbons in my hair . . . yuck! My first summer in California is going to be my worst summer ever, anywhere.

I want to shout and scream and stomp my feet, but I bury that feeling way, way down in my stomach.

I still have one chance. Last-ditch effort.

"Okay, I'm going, Dad," I say through my gritted teeth.

"Do your homework when you come back," he says.

Ugh! I want to scream! He's so stupid! "I don't have any homework. Tomorrow's the second-to-last day of school." I must say it in a really snotty way, because he tells me to go take my walk and change my attitude. I haven't heard that in a long time.

I'd be happy to change my attitude, but it's pretty hard with things like this going on behind my back! "Come on, Toby," I say. He runs to me excitedly with his tongue hanging out. At least he's happy. I'm glad someone is.

I need to calm down, so I walk farther with Toby than I usually do. I walk all the way through the meadow where Madison, Sam, and I did our Siren Call and continue on the dirt path. I breathe in and breathe out. I think about Dad with Terri instead of Paige, my friendship with Madison, Larry liking Samantha instead of me. I keep breathing in and out, in and out. Sounds of people come and go—conversations, games, babies crying. Traffic passes, but it sounds very far away. Breathe in, breathe out. Suddenly I find myself on the opposite side of the lake, looking across at our house. I only ever walk this far when Dad and I walk around the whole lake together. I've never been here by myself.

I find a quiet spot, far from people passing by, and sit on the grass by the edge of the water. Toby sits beside me and we breathe in and out together—though his breathing has a more slobbery sound.

Before I send my message in a bottle to the universe, I have one more thing to say, and I want to put it in writing.

I unzip all the zippers of my backpack, looking for a pen. I find a short, stubby pencil from when Dad and I played miniature golf back when we first moved here. I can't find even the smallest scrap of paper anywhere—who uses paper anymore?—but luckily there's a crumpled napkin from a time Dad treated me to some fast food. There's a little smudge of ketchup on the napkin, but otherwise it's clean. I don't think the universe will mind.

Dear Universe,

If Ryder Landry can help bring me and Madison together, please bring him.

If you or anyone can bring sense to my dad, please bring it!

And don't worry about me anymore. If Larry likes me, so what? I'll deal with it.

Work on those other things if you can. Thanks!

Your friend, Cleo Nelson

I roll the napkin up tightly and put it in the wine bottle with the letter.

I give the bottle a little kiss—a friend kiss, not a romantic one—and throw it into the water. Toby jumps up and barks once, excited by the splash. I turn around, satisfied. Maybe I contacted the universe. Maybe I achieved something special. If not, at least I tried.

"Hey, did you throw trash into the lake?" a voice shouts.

Oh no! It's Red Shorts—again! He's over on the path, walking in place. Why is he around every time I try to call the universe?

He seems just as surprised to see me. "You again?"

Toby barks angrily now and runs toward the man. I grab his leash before he can get too close, but Toby thinks Red Shorts is up to no good and pulls me along.

My first instinct is to pull Toby in the opposite direction, run and get home as fast as humanly possible, avoid Dad at his computer, and hide in my room. But today, after all my breathing in and out and my summoning of the universe, I have courage. I walk over toward the man, who's walking in place and unzipping the sack on his butt to get to his phone.

"It wasn't trash. I was doing something very special. Almost spiritual," I tell him. I glance out at the lake. The bottle is slowly floating away. "And I promise I'll never do it again."

"Well, that's interesting," he says. "If it wasn't trash, what was it?"

Right now, I don't care who knows. "It was a message in a bottle."

Still moving his feet up and down like he's walking, he looks at his phone but doesn't dial. "What kind of message?" he asks.

"It's a private matter." I'm acting all mature, but on the inside I'm a scared, squalling baby.

He smiles. "A love note?"

"No. Not really. I mean, I *did* write to a boy, but it wasn't a boy I want as a boyfriend; it was . . . well, a famous boy, and for some reason—and I'm not really even sure why or how anymore—I'm thinking that he could make everything right between me and a friend of mine." All these words come gushing out of my mouth like a waterfall. I have no control over it. But I can't stop. I guess I really want to tell someone all of this, and who better than this stranger who never stops walking? He's here, he's listening, and he doesn't seem to be judging—not yet. So I go on, whether he wants me to or not. At least as I'm talking, he's not dialing the police.

"But I also wrote to the universe because I want my dad and his girlfriend—well, his ex-girlfriend—to get back together because she's his *Only One* and I know it, maybe because they weren't a lovey-dovey boyfriend and girlfriend, the kind that make you wanna go *blech* and throw up. They had fun together; they seemed like friends, and now he's going to marry Paige even though he's never looked like he's friends with her. She's another friend's mom, though I'm not sure whether Sam is a friend or not, but that's another story and"—I take a breath—"I guess, if you really want to know, it wasn't a love note. You could maybe call it a friendship note."

Red Shorts looks thoughtful. "Friendship is just as important as love," he says.

"Really?" I ask. "It seems like all anybody talks about anymore is love, love, love. I'm kind of sick of it."

He laughs. "I know what you mean. It's best when you have both: love and friendship. My wife—she was my best friend. A person like that is hard to find."

Without even thinking about it, I'm walking in place with him, I guess to keep him company. "I think my mom was my dad's best friend, but she died a long time ago," I tell him.

"I'm sorry to hear that."

"I'm sorry about your wife too," I say.

And for just a couple of seconds, he stops walking. "Thank you. That's very nice of you to say." His feet start moving again. "What's your name?" he asks.

"Cleo."

"Nice to meet you, Cleo. My name's Tim."

"Nice to meet you, Tim."

"I'd better go," he says. "I hope your dad finds a new best friend."

"I hope you do too," I say. Then he smiles and jogs off.

20

Everyone knows there's no learning on the last day of school, but at Friendship Community there's no learning on the second-to-last day of school either. Because the Bling Bling Summer Fling is tonight, all the kids are as unfocused as I am on a normal day. The school is filled with this jumpy, electric energy. Everyone is buzzing.

Like all teachers, Kevin can sense kids having a good time and, of course, bring an end to it. He does this with five terrible words:

"Time for your book reports!"

Oh no!

Everyone in the classroom starts opening their desks and backpacks to pull out the books they've read, while my eyes dart around the room in a panic. How come no one reminded me? Madison never mentioned her book; neither did Samantha. Even my "boyfriend," Larry, could've brought up working on his report, but did he? No!

Or maybe they did and I had other things on my mind. Who knows?

As my classmates get up and talk about their spy thrillers, their vampire love stories, and their futuristic adventures, I sit and worry. What could I possibly say about my book? I did try to read it a couple of times, but it barely made sense from the very first paragraph. I don't even have it in my backpack, so I can't cheat—like some of the kids are doing—and just read a page or two out loud. What am I going to—?

"Cleo." Kevin's voice interrupts my thoughts. "Come on up and tell us about your book."

I sit in my chair a moment longer. I see Larry smiling, eager to hear what I have to say. Samantha looks at me with her eyebrows scrunched together, worried. And Madison nods encouragingly. Easy for her to do—her report was about a teenage detective named Lucy Lindelow, and it sounded totally fun! How did she wind up with *that* book?

I slowly stand and walk to the front of the room. I give Kevin an apologetic look. "I don't have my book with me."

"That's okay," he says. "Tell us about it."

"It doesn't have an interesting cover anyway. No pictures," I tell the class. Then I take a breath. "Anyway, the book I read is called *Quantum Physics, Biocentrism, and the Universe as We Know It.*"

I look out at the faces. The ones who are paying attention at all look totally confused. "Wow," says Kevin. "How much of that did you understand?"

I decide to be honest. "Not a lot. I would read a paragraph again and again, and it could have been Portuguese or Chinese or Martian. It made no sense at all."

"I'm not surprised," Kevin says. "So, did you learn anything from trying?"

"A little," I say. I look out at Lisa Lee, who is concentrating on picking something from underneath her fingernail. Madison looks unsure of where this is going. "Quantum physics doesn't seem to be like chemistry, where you can experiment with different types of matter and see specific cool results. But it's still scientists trying to understand the universe down to its tiniest, tiniest particles. For years they thought the universe worked one way; then they realized they were wrong."

Larry watches me, nodding. I think he's trying to look interested, but as smart as he is, I'm sure he's as confused as the rest of them.

"What I learned is that you can be the smartest scientist in the world, but particles and waves and protons and neutrons can't explain coincidences, or who becomes friends, or who falls in love."

At that, people ooh and aah and Ronnie Cheseboro

pumps his fist in the air and shouts, "Woot woot!" (whatever that means). Maybe I shouldn't have mentioned love.

I decide I'd better finish up. "So I guess what I learned from this book is that scientists can try, and they can think they have the answers, but someone can always come around years later and change it. Nobody's ever going to be able to explain everything in the universe." I pause. "And that's it."

As I walk back to my desk, I see Lisa Lee looking at whatever she got out from under her fingernail. "She's not getting credit for that, is she?" She's sort of asking Kevin and sort of just saying it.

"Yes," says Kevin. "Cleo took on a tough subject, and she should be commended for it."

Larry applauds and whistles—not wildly, just to be nice. Sam joins him for a clap or two. Out of the corner of my eye, I see Madison look at Lisa Lee and shrug.

For the rest of the day, the topic goes back to tonight's Bling Bling Summer Fling. I'm not filled with the enthusiasm and anticipation everyone else has; for me it's all awkwardness and discomfort. At lunchtime, Madison says "hi" when she sees me, Samantha, and Larry, but she still walks past us and sits with Lisa Lee, Kylie Mae, Ronnie, and Lonnie.

Every conversation I overhear is about the Bling Bling. Who's going with who. Whose parents are driving. "What time are you getting there?" "What are you wearing?" "Did you hear about the new ride?" "This is going to be the best one ever!"

Blah blah blah. By the end of the day, I'm sick of the Bling Bling Summer Fling, and it hasn't even happened yet.

Waiting for Dad to pick me up in the school parking lot, I've convinced myself I don't feel well. It's not just in my head; I think it's in my body too, for real. My stomach feels gross, my face feels hot, and all I want to do is lie in bed.

"Are you excited for the Bling Bling?"

Madison's voice comes from behind me, asking the last question I want to hear, from someone I don't really want to talk to. But she's cornered me at a time when I have nowhere to go, no way to get away.

"Uh, I don't know," I say. "I'm not feeling so great."

"You'll feel better once you get there. Hollywoodland Park is so fun; you're gonna love it."

"Yeah, maybe." Or maybe not.

"I haven't had a chance to tell you." She pauses. "I'm going with Lisa Lee and Kylie Mae." She pauses again. I wonder why. Did she expect me to gasp? To clutch at my heart and fall to the ground?

I don't do anything. I stand there stone-faced. Finally I say, "I heard."

"I've been wanting to tell you the last day or two."

"Yeah, I figured." I stretch my neck and look at the far end of the parking lot. No sign of Dad.

Madison looks past me and says "hey" to Samantha and Larry, who have come up behind me. Larry nods and Sam gives a little wave, but they keep their distance. They don't join our conversation. *Conversation,* though, might not be the right word for what Madison and I are having. I'm just letting her talk and responding as simply as possible because it would be rude not to.

"Our parents are kind of *making* us go together," Madison tells me. I haven't asked her for an explanation of why she's deserting me on the most important night of the whole school year for people who are friends, but here she goes. "It's tradition. Our parents like going together too. It doesn't have anything to do with you."

I nod. I don't think Madison is lying exactly, but I also don't totally believe her. It's a weird feeling.

"I mean, we're still friends. I mean, you and I are still friends. For sure. But I'm kind of friends with them too. They've just wanted to hang out for the last few days of the school year, and it's hard to be friends with everybody at the same time."

I stay silent. I wouldn't know how hard it is to have so many friends that I don't have time for all of them. "We can get together during the summer just like we planned," Madison says. "Before I go to Hawaii. And when I get back.

And seventh grade will be cool. I'll have it all figured out by then."

I'm still looking for Dad's car when I see the Paddingtons' SUV pull into the parking lot. "Yvonne's here," I tell Madison. Inside my head, I thank Yvonne in all two languages I know: *thanks and* gracias.

"Oh shoot, she texted that she needs to get me home fast today. But I'll look for you at the Bling Bling. We'll talk more there." Madison jumps into the SUV, and Yvonne drives off.

There's one moment of silence before I hear Sam's voice. "Did you believe any of that?"

I feel my shoulders slump as I turn around.

"Not really," I say.

"I think she'll be nice to us, at least," Larry says.

"Yeah," Sam agrees. "It's not going to go back to the way it used to be. She's a nicer person now. She's just going to stick where she belongs."

"Right," I say. "With Lisa Lee and Kylie Mae. In Hawaii."

"And at the Bling Bling," Samantha says. "But don't worry, we'll have fun there too."

No, we won't, I think. *Not if I'm home in bed.*

On the way home, I tell Dad that I'm not feeling well.

"But tonight's the Bling Bling Summer Fling!" he says, like he's personally excited about it.

"So what? It's gonna be dumb." For sure Dad doesn't want to spend a Thursday night at an amusement park surrounded by screaming kids. He'd rather be at home with a book, or working on his wedding website. *Save the Date! Paige and I Are Going to Be the Happiest Couple in the World!* Barf.

"Dumb? It's not gonna be dumb at all," Dad says. "From everything I've heard, it's the biggest event of the social season; it's the pinnacle of what the universe has to offer."

I just stare at him. He knows the look.

"Okay, I'm exaggerating," he says with a smile. "But we've heard about Hollywoodland Park forever. Don't you want to check it out for yourself?"

I shrug. "Not really."

"Well, we don't have to leave for a couple of hours. Let's see how you feel then."

I know how I'll feel. Just like I do now.

At home, I lie in bed. Every once in a while I turn over on my stomach and look at my magazines with Ryder Landry in them. "It's not your fault I feel like this," I say to Ryder. Toby looks up, thinking I was talking to him. "And nothing's ever your fault, Tobes!" I say, patting him on the head.

Around six, our doorbell rings, and Toby runs out my door. I'm hoping Dad gave up on the idea of the Bling Bling and ordered in some food. I could go for pepperoni pizza right about now. That makes everything a little better, at least.

A minute later my bedroom door opens and Sam bursts through, shouting, "¡*Hola, amiga!* Surprise!"

"What are you doing here?"

"We wanted to surprise you, especially because you were so bummed out about Madison. We're all going to Hollywoodland Park together!"

"All?" I ask.

"Yeah, all of us," Sam says. "Your dad. My mom. Me. You. Larry."

"Larry?" I ask. The last thing I need is to be on a "date" with Larry tonight, sitting close to each other on roller coasters and water rides, in front of the rest of the school—all the people who remember him as Scabby Larry, which wasn't that long ago.

"He's in your living room bonding with Toby right now." And as if he's in a play and heard his cue, Toby runs into my room, with Larry clomping behind him.

"Hey, Cleo, cool house! I love your dog . . . and all your dad's computers." Right now, though, his super-alert eyes are taking in everything in my room from floor to ceiling. "Your room is fun too. Except for that!" he says, pointing at a Ryder poster on my wall. "Ugh! I couldn't go to sleep with that creepo-teen-robot staring over me."

"But he's okay with bikini models," Sam tells me.

"She saw *one* picture of a bikini model on my notebook,

and she hasn't been quiet about it since!" says Larry. They poke at each other, giggling. They were acting this way at lunch too, with the monkey.

"Whose idea was this, anyway?" I ask.

"I don't know exactly," Samantha says. "Your dad's or my mom's. One of them. They've been talking about it for a week or two. Ever since the art show."

They've been talking about a lot more than that, I think. I guess Samantha doesn't know about their wedding plans either. We're going to be sisters and she doesn't even know. A couple of months ago, that would have made us as happy as Lisa Lee with a new suede jacket. Now, after all this time, it's going to happen whether we want it to or not, when all I really want to be is friends. Real friends, not forced sisters.

"Come on, let's get out of here!" Sam suddenly shouts. "You're not sick. You're bummed out, and that can be fixed with three words!"

"Claws . . . of . . . Doom!" Larry and Sam say together; then they both laugh. That must be one of the rides at the park.

"I hope you'll protect me if I get scared," says Larry, cozying up to Sam.

She pushes him away, saying, "Get outta here!" But she's got a big smile on her face.

"Fine. Whatever you say, dearest!" he jokes. "Come on, Toby, let's go look at the computers!" Larry runs out of my room with Toby following.

I listen to them making noise all the way down the hall as I stare at Samantha, confused. When Larry is far enough away, I say, "What is going on with you two?"

Samantha doesn't answer. She just lifts her fingers to her neck and moves the collar of her shirt away.

Her necklace is gone!

"You asked the universe for Larry?" I ask.

Sam looks down, her face getting a little red. "Well . . . yeah. I didn't know if I should because I thought maybe you liked him. You *said* you didn't, but you were dancing with him in Focus! and hugging him in chemistry. Then you had his monkey at the lake and I thought you *really* must like him . . . but then you didn't throw it in. It's been really hard to figure out what you've been up to lately, Cleo."

Wow, I never thought the things *I* did would confuse anyone. I thought the whole point of my life was to be confused by everyone else!

"So, is he your boyfriend now?" I ask Sam.

"Welllllll," she says, shifting from one foot to the other, "I don't know if he's my *boyfriend* exactly, but I like having him around. Maybe we'll see tonight."

"So what was the offering *you* threw in the lake? He didn't . . . *use* that toilet paper, like, on his butt, did he?" I mean, I have to ask.

"Ewww, no!" Sam screeches. "The offering was *in* the toilet paper."

"I didn't see anything."

"Well . . ." She pauses. She's wondering whether to tell me or not. "It always worked with voodoo."

I immediately know. "His hair? You plucked a piece of hair out of his head and he didn't notice?"

"Nah, it was even easier than that. I spotted it on the back of his shirt and voilà! Offering to the universe."

This is hard to believe. "And your necklace really just *fell* off?"

"Maybe." She rolls her eyes a little, then smiles. "Or maybe I gave it a little tug."

"Kids, let's get ready to go!" It's not Dad's voice shouting from the front of the house; it's Paige's. I guess it's a sound I need to get used to. Samantha runs out my door, shouting for me to follow.

Dad doesn't want me to stay home at all, and he's definitely not going to let me stay home alone. I'm going, because I'd never be able to explain to Dad and Paige and Sam and Larry all the reasons why I *don't* want to go, that I'm not interested in Blinging and Flinging with the rest of them. I will not participate, though. I quickly fill my backpack with drawing pads and colored pencils. They'll entertain me. I'll do my own thing. I'll be a loner. I'm going, but I'll be hanging out with the only person in this world I seem to understand—myself.

"Cleo, come on! We're leaving!" Dad shouts.

But I've got to do one more thing before I go.

It's not going to be done out of sadness, or anger, or even

because I'm discouraged and bummed out. It just needs to be done.

I stand in front of my mirror and lift my scissors to my neck. I carefully put the sharp edges on either side of the frayed string. I snip.

The necklace falls down my body and onto my dresser, the shell clunking softly against the wood, landing right next to the empty bottle of love potion.

There's just no point in wearing it anymore. The universe might be listening, but it's doing whatever it wants.

21

Paige drives to Hollywoodland Park with Dad in the passenger seat, making us a normal little "family." I keep my eyes open for anything romantic between Dad and Paige, but luckily Paige keeps both hands on the steering wheel, and they talk about how the school is always asking them for money and other boring things. No wedding plans. Not in front of us, anyway.

There's plenty of room in the back for us kids, especially since Sam and Larry are sitting closer than they need to. The sides of their butts almost touch each other, and whenever the car hits a bump, Larry bounces into Samantha, who acts like it bothers her. She knocks him with her hip and tells him to stay in his own area. I stare out the window at the passing freeway scenery (fast food, billboard, more fast food) to avoid paying too much attention.

"Hey, this was all your idea," Larry teases Sam. "You're the one who checked the box marked 'YES'!"

That comment turns my head around.

"Checked 'YES'?" I ask. "What does that mean?"

"Oh, my little sister started doing this dumb thing," Larry tells me. "I think she liked some boy, so she was writing on every piece of paper she could find, 'DO YOU LIKE ME? YES OR NO. CHECK ONE.' I finally just started using them for scratch paper and projects and stuff. I told Sam about it and she thought it was funny, so I gave one to her as a joke."

"And to me!" I say. I probably shouldn't, not when Larry and Sam look so happy together in their bizarre little two-person world, but I can't help myself.

"You?" he asks.

"The rocket you launched at outdoor break. The one you asked me to pick up."

Larry looks at me like Toby does when I pretend to throw a ball but hide it behind my back instead—totally mystified. And much like Toby, he doesn't seem to have anything to say.

Is Larry going to make me explain it? In front of Sam? I don't necessarily want to, but I need answers, so I don't have any other choice. "Inside the rocket. It said that. DO YOU LIKE ME? YES OR NO."

Larry shakes his head like he's never heard of such a

thing. "I didn't notice. Maybe my sister wrote on it [and] taped it up."

If a lightning bolt came out of the sky and hit m[e] now in Paige's car, I couldn't be more shocked. "Wha[t about] my pencil case? When it exploded with all the conf[etti?"

"I did that," Sam says. She must see the sur[prise on] my face. "You seemed kind of down, and I wanted [to cheer] you up."

"But we were hardly even friends then."

She shrugs. "I wanted to be."

"So did I! But then why were you mean to me i[n class] and stuff?"

Samantha's face looks like it's searching for the [answer] to that question. "I don't know," she says. "I couldn['t think] of any other way to act. Then at the art show, I saw [we] could maybe work together again. And be friends."

"Then it all worked out, didn't it? I love it when [life] has a happy ending!" Larry jokes. But if this were [a story,] it would have a complicated ending, not a happ[y one.] Larry didn't write me the note in the rocket . . . o[r the] confetti bomb to go off in my pencil case . . . wh[o wrote] the note Lisa Lee picked up in the lunch line?

Could she have planted it there on the floor he[rself?]

But Larry also wanted me for his partner in squ[ar danc-]ing . . . he said he loved me . . . he acted . . . he ac[ted . . .]

Maybe he was acting like he always did. A[nd]

233

thought it was something else, making it into something bigger in my own mind.

It all sounds pretty unbelievable, but it's hard for me to believe that anything's unbelievable anymore.

So I'll believe it . . . I guess.

After about forty minutes of driving, Paige practically sings, "Look, kids, we're he-ere!" It's not like we need an announcement. We can see it with our own eyes: big letters spelling out "Hollywoodland" over a parking lot that goes on for miles.

Right away I recognize the big yellow roller coaster with cars designed to look like rockets from a science-fiction movie. We're close enough to hear the cranking noise of it going uphill, and the distant shouts and screams of people having fun.

When we get inside the park, the first thing Sam and Larry want to do is have their picture taken in a little shop where you dress up like old-timey movie characters. They ask if I want to join, and I say no.

"Are you still pretending you don't feel well?" Dad asks.

"Cleo, you don't feel well?" Paige asks, putting her hand on my forehead. I pull away. I don't need anyone checking my temperature, especially not Samantha's mom!

"No, she's just lackluster," Dad tells Paige. "I think the end of the school year is a letdown for her."

"Really?" Paige sounds surprised. "When I was in school, I was always dying for the year to end!"

"Maybe you didn't like learning," I say under my breath, but Dad hears me loud and clear.

"Cleo," he warns me. "Don't talk like that to . . . Samantha's mom."

He paused. He was about to say *"my girlfriend"*! He was about to say *"my fiancée"*! He was about to say *"the woman who's going to be your mom, whether you like it or not"*!

"Sorry," I mumble, not meaning it but knowing it's the right thing to say. As Paige takes Sam and Larry to the photo shop, I tell Dad that I'm just not feeling this Bling Bling stuff. I came along because I wanted to see what it was like, but now that I've seen it, I really just want to work on my latest drawings.

"You can do that all summer," Dad says.

Yeah, in between wedding plans.

"Are you sure you don't want to go on one of the rides?" he asks.

With Larry and Samantha on their date? With Dad and Paige on theirs? No thanks! "No. Not right now."

I can tell Dad is about to ask me another question, but a voice stops him. "Hi, Mr. Nelson! Hi, Cleo!"

It's Madison. With Lisa Lee and Kylie Mae at her side.

Dad says hello to Madison, then of course acts like a total dork by saying to Lisa Lee and Kylie Mae, "I haven't heard about you girls before, but any friends of Cleo's are friends of mine." They're all friendliness and smiles as they say hello, but all I'm thinking is *Be quiet, Dad, be quiet quiet quiet!*

"I told you we'd see you here!" Madison says happily. "I've been wanting to tell you . . . I wasn't sure before, but tonight I found out . . ."

Lisa Lee, who's reading a text, taps Madison on the shoulder. "We've got to go. My dad's almost at the front of the VIP line at the Claws of Doom, and we can get in with him."

Madison nods. "I'll talk to you later, okay?" she says to me. "See ya, Mr. Nelson!" Then she runs off with her two best friends as I stand in the middle of California's favorite amusement park . . . with my dad.

"They seem nice," he says. "Are they some new friends?"

"No, they've known each other their whole lives," I grumble.

"I meant, are they new friends of yours?"

"Not really."

Dad doesn't ask anything else because Samantha and Larry and Paige return from the photo shop, all pumped up about the fun they had. They show me the picture: Sam's in a long, frilly gown with a feather in her hair like the owner of an 1800s saloon, and Larry's in a cowboy hat and vest. There's even a fake horse in the background.

They ask me to go with them to ride the rides, but Dad tells them I don't feel very well (which is nice of him, since he knows it's not true). They head off with Paige, who says she'll see my dad later. She'll see him later, all right. For the rest of her life.

Dad buys me a funnel cake with extra powdered sugar, then lets me do what I want—sit on a bench and draw. I tell him to go have fun with Paige and Sam and Larry, but he's happy to sit nearby and read a book on his tablet. That's fine by me, as long as he keeps his distance so I *feel* like I'm alone.

It's starting to get a little dark out, but there are plenty of bright streetlights inside the park, so I position myself underneath one. When my funnel cake is gone, I can still breathe in and smell popcorn and corn dogs and cotton candy. Everywhere around me people are screaming and laughing and having fun, but on my drawing pad, Panda-roo is tired, settling in for a long nap. His cave is filled with the latest gadgets and surveillance systems, though, so if anything goes wrong in the universe, he'll wake up. It takes a while to draw all the details, so I don't know how long it's been when I hear a shout of "Cleo!" in the distance.

It's Samantha, walking back toward me with her mom and Larry. They all have big smiles, red faces, and slightly messed-up hair—even Paige, who's always perfect. They must have ridden the Scrambler or the Log Flume or those swings that go around and around in a circle until you want to throw up.

"We know you're not in the mood for rides," Sam says,

"but there's this amphitheater in the park where they do shows every hour. Magicians and jugglers and things."

Dad must have heard them from his bench, because now he's standing over me too, saying, "That sounds neat."

"Lame," I say, looking down at my drawing pad.

"We think so too," says Larry. "That's why it might be fun. We need a break from the rides. My stomach doesn't feel so great; I need to sit for a while."

"Let's check it out," Dad says. "You can still sit and draw. We won't bother you; we'll just be near you."

The bench is starting to feel hard against my butt anyway, so I decide to go. It's not quite eight o'clock, so the amphitheater isn't full yet. We take some seats a few rows from the stage, and I put my nose right back into my drawing pad while all the lovebirds chat. After a few minutes pass, people start filling up the place—kids and adults who must also need a break from the flipping and flying and bouncing they've been doing for the last hour or two.

Out of the corner of my eye, I see Sam and Larry poking and shoving each other. They seem more like friends—or joking enemies—than girlfriend and boyfriend. I can also tell that Dad's not paying very much attention to Paige. His eyes are moving all around the amphitheater like he's looking for someone else. That doesn't seem like a nice way to treat your fiancée, but it's none of my business, so I keep my mouth shut.

Suddenly there's a big, loud drumroll, and a voice

announces, "Ladies and gentlemen, boys and girls, porcupines and octopi, arachnids and animals . . ."

Porcupines and octopi *are* animals. Oh boy, this is going to be bad.

"Thank you for being a part of our Hollywoodland Park family tonight. We hope you are ready for an evening of fun and excitement, action and laughter! So sit back, relax, and enjoy the show!"

Loud, goofy, prerecorded music plays, and everyone watches as four clowns run onstage and start tumbling and falling down and generally being dumb and clowny. They're followed by a juggler making dopey jokes and only juggling balls—nothing cool like torches of fire or chainsaws. I start opening my backpack to attempt drawing in the dark as the juggler leaves the stage to applause.

The stage is quiet for a moment until another announcement comes out of the way-too-loud loudspeakers. "Ladies and gentlemen, boys and girls, fruit flies and bald eagles . . ."

Oh no, this again.

"Tonight we have a surprise guest, and I know he'll be a big hit with the kids out there. . . ."

As big a hit as the clowns and the juggler? I think. Then I feel kind of bad. Just because I'm not in a good mood doesn't mean they're not decent performers. It's not their fault I'm here without a date and that my friend Madison—now former friend, I guess—is here with her real friends.

The announcer continues over the loudspeakers. "He

only has time for a couple of songs, because this is his last appearance before his tour of Asia. . . ."

Tour of Asia? No, it couldn't be!

"Ryderrrrrrr . . ."

Oh my gosh, *could* it really be?

"Lannnnnnnndry!"

No way. It can't be.

But it is.

22

The music from "Love Monsoon" fills the amphitheater as Ryder Landry runs onstage. I've seen that run in clip after clip online—live performances, music videos, even news stories where he's running from fans. It's the best run ever.

"Hello, Southern California—it's the end of the school year! Woooo!" he shouts into the microphone. Everyone in the audience goes crazy—except me. I don't know what to think or how to act. I feel like someone conked me over the head with a big, heavy frying pan. My brain is scrambled.

I stand up without even realizing it. I look over at Dad, who's smiling at me. "This is the guy! Right?" he asks, shouting over the screams and cheers. I don't say anything, still in shock. But I'm sure Dad gets his answer from Sam, who is jumping up and down and screaming, "Oh my gosh oh my gosh oh my gosh!" Even Larry is standing, and he thinks Ryder Landry is a creepo-teen-robot who won't be around in five years' time.

"I hope you don't mind that I'm singing to a backing track tonight. My band's already on their way to Japan. But before I left, I wanted to do a special favor for a friend."

A favor . . . for a friend? That's how I signed my letter! Still, it couldn't be because of me . . . could it? I'm clenching my hands so tightly that my nails are digging into my palms.

"So buckle up and get ready for a love monsoon!" Ryder shouts as his music cranks up again.

I mouth the words as Ryder sings—or maybe I scream the words at the top of my lungs; I really have no idea. It's hard to pry my eyes away from Ryder, in his skinny jeans and white T-shirt with suspenders and a knit beanie, but a few times I crane my neck and look left, right, and behind us. Whether this has anything to do with me or not, I hope, hope, *hope* Madison is here to enjoy it!

The applause after "Love Monsoon" seems endless, but Ryder quiets everyone down with a wave of his hand. He says he's only here for a couple of songs, so my heart jumps out of my chest when the next song is "I Like You, Baby." My favorite! Well, one of my *many* favorites!

I'm jumping up and down in place without really realizing it while kids are gathering in front of the stage to dance. I don't even mean to take my eyes away from Ryder—who knows when I'll see him in person again, if ever?—but somehow my eye wanders down to the crowd and glimpses a flash of blond hair—Madison's!

I'm so glad she's here. Even if she *is* dancing with Lisa Lee and Kylie Mae.

Then I see her wave to me. I wave back. But she's not just waving hello; she's waving for me to come down and join them.

"Is she . . . ?" I ask Samantha, but Sam's already moving toward the end of the row, pulling me and Larry with her. I look to Dad for permission, and he nods.

Samantha, Larry, and I squeeze through the crowd. As Ryder sings and dances and encourages the audience to join in (which of course we do), we make our way toward Madison. Lisa Lee and Kylie Mae are smiling as they watch Ryder, and when their attention turns to us . . . they keep on smiling! I've never seen anything like it. It's almost as big a surprise as Ryder Landry was.

When the song ends on a big, loud high note, it seems like the screaming and cheering will never end. Ryder smiles and waves until we quiet down again; then he says, "I only have time for one more song."

There are sighs, "awws," and a couple of friendly boos. Only Larry says "yay," but it's obviously a joke. Samantha and Madison both punch him from opposite sides.

"All of my songs mean something to me," he tells the audience as he walks back and forth. "But this one has special meaning, especially for kids like us. And if there's one thing I've learned, in all the places I've traveled and from all the awesome people I've met, it's that there's nothing more important than friendship."

I totally agree! I guess everyone else does too, because they cheer like crazy. And the cheers get even louder when we hear the first notes of "Friend to the End of the Earth."

"I'm a man who lives for love."

The crowd screeches and squeals.

"Love fits me like a glove
But love like that can come and go.
When I need to talk, or take that long, long
  walk
You're the one who won't say no.
Because you're my friend, my friend
My friend to the end of the Earth."

I look over at Madison. Her eyes are glistening with tears. Is it my fault she's crying? I wanted Ryder to help bring us back together, but I didn't want her to cry. She puts her arms out toward Lisa Lee and Kylie Mae, who immediately lean in for a group hug. Their three heads bop up and down in time to Ryder's song.

Well, that's it. Madison has made her choice. She's got

two friends to the end of the Earth, and there's no room for a third.

It feels like someone has grabbed my heart and squeezed it hard. Suddenly this great Ryder song about friendship sounds like the saddest thing in the world to me. Even Ryder Landry himself can't hold me in place. I can't stand on the sidelines looking at Madison and her friends one second longer. I turn my back to the stage and walk away, clenching my teeth together and trying not to cry.

With my eyes closed, I hear Ryder shout, "Good night, Southern California!" to the crowd. "Have a great summer, and I'll see you soon!"

The music fades out, and everyone screams and cheers and shouts his name. Everyone but me, that is. Then he must be gone for good, because I start to hear kids talking and feel people walking past me. I breathe in and out, trying to get my emotions under control. An amazing thing just happened, and I may have had something to do with it. But that doesn't even matter anymore. What should have been one of the happiest moments of my life turned out to be one of the worst.

Someone taps me on the shoulder. I turn. It's Lisa Lee, with Kylie Mae by her side. "Did that really just happen?" Lisa Lee asks.

I gulp and force a half smile. "I was just wondering that too," I say.

"I think it did," Kylie Mae says.

We all look at each other for a moment. Our conversation seems to be over, but when I really think about it, it's probably the nicest conversation we've ever had.

A second later, before I can barely see her coming, I've almost been tackled—by Madison. She throws her arms around me and hugs me tight. The sadness is knocked right out of me. Confusion has taken over.

"I'm gonna miss you so much!" she says. Miss me? When? This summer? The rest of my life?

When Madison lets me go, she sees I'm standing with Lisa Lee and Kylie Mae. "I'm glad you guys are talking! I just invited Sam. . . ." Sam is standing with us too, grinning wildly. "But I haven't gotten to tell you about the sleepover yet."

"What?" I ask. "What sleepover?"

"I've been begging for days, but my mom and dad are finally going to let me have a campout in the backyard tomorrow night. A big last-day-of-school party and sleepover, and then on Saturday we can play in the pool and have a barbecue."

I look around at Madison's two sets of friends: me and Samantha, Lisa Lee and Kylie Mae. "*All* of us?" I ask.

"Yes!" she says. "I've wanted to tell you about it, but I wasn't sure until tonight. We leave for Hawaii next week, but I hope we can have a lot of fun until then!"

I look at Samantha with her goofy smile. We both nod.

Of course we want to have as much fun as possible at Madison's house before she leaves for Hawaii. But can it really be true? Could we really *all* be friends? I guess there's only one way to find out, and that starts with a sleepover.

Larry interrupts. "I'm really excited about this party, ladies. . . ."

"You're not invited!" Madison and Samantha shout together.

"Good," he says. "I don't want to be there anyway if you're playing *his* music." He sneers up at the stage, but we know he's kidding. "I just want to say that it's time to ride the Claws of Doom!"

"We've already been, but I'll go again," Lisa Lee says. "My dad can get us to the front."

"Can we come too?" Larry asks.

Lisa Lee looks at Kylie Mae. I don't see an expression cross either of their faces, but something must be communicated between them because Lisa Lee says, "I guess." It's not in the nicest tone I've ever heard, but at least it's the right words!

"Yes!" Sam says, psyched. "See you later!" They all run up the aisle toward their parents, while Madison and I stand together.

"You don't want to go on the Claws of Doom?" she asks.

"Yeah, I guess. But I also don't want to leave. I could stare at this stage forever." Then I say the obvious. "I can't believe what just happened."

"I know," Madison says, looking up at the stage too, her hand absentmindedly going to her neck.

And that's when I notice it. Her necklace is gone, just like Sam's! "Did you pull off your necklace too?" I ask her.

"No, you won't believe this! It fell off today after school."

I gasp in surprise. "Oh my gosh, the universe actually heard your Siren Call? You wished for Ryder and he appeared!"

"Well, the universe heard me," she says seriously, "but Ryder wasn't my wish."

I don't understand. "He wasn't? Who was it, then?"

"It was all of us," she says. She must see the confusion on my face. "Remember the badge I threw into the lake?"

I nod. "Yeah, from the concert you went to with Lisa Lee and Kylie Mae."

"Right. And you and Samantha love Ryder too. I was using the Ryder badge to wish for all of us to be friends."

"Then . . . maybe it worked."

"Who knows?" Madison says with a smile.

"Only the universe!" I say. "It's always listening."

"But it's not talking!" Madison gives me a hug. "Come on and meet us at the Claws of Doom, okay?"

"Okay," I say, still a little stunned by everything that's happened. I watch her run off; then I walk back to the benches where all of this began. Sam and Larry are trying to drag Paige to the Claws of Doom while Dad types something into his phone. When he looks up and sees me, he says, "Well, that was quite the surprise!"

"Yeah, it was fun." I'm acting all casual but inside I'm bursting. It was only a day I'll remember for the rest of my life!

"That was pretty cool, I guess," Larry says, and I decide I'll wait until tomorrow to give him a hard time about knowing all of Ryder Landry's lyrics. "But right now we've got to go to the Claws of Doom."

"Woo-hoo!" Samantha shouts. "Let's go!"

Her mom is not as enthusiastic, but she sighs and says, "Okay." She turns to my dad, whose phone has just dinged with a text, and asks, "Has she tracked you down yet?"

Dad looks up toward the entrance to the amphitheater. "I believe she has." I follow his eyes, but all I see is the backs of people's heads bobbing up and down—the big crowd still leaving the show.

Then I see a face coming in the other direction, toward us. A smiling face topped with long red hair.

Terri?

23

Terri is jostled by the crowd leaving the amphitheater but makes her way through. "Glad I found you!" she shouts as she heads down the aisle. She says hi to all of us and gives Dad a hug. Then he gives her a kiss! Just a quick little smooch, but it was on the lips, so it's not something he should be doing in front of Paige.

"What are you doing here?" I ask.

"I like roller coasters," she says. She puts an arm around Dad and squeezes the back of his neck, like she used to do when they were a couple. What is going on?

Dad explains without me asking out loud. "Terri wanted to come with us tonight, but she knew she'd be late. That's why Paige drove."

"So you're not on a date?" My eyes dart from Dad to Paige and back to Dad.

"No!" he says. "I haven't been on a date since Terri and I broke up."

Again I look back and forth from Dad to Paige. "You're not getting married?"

"Married?" yells just about everyone.

Terri laughs and looks at Dad. "What haven't you told me?"

"Dad's been working on the website!" Maybe I shouldn't be saying this in front of Terri, but I can't help myself. "I've seen it on his computer! There are doves and cakes and bells, and it says 'Save the Date'!"

Samantha's mom interrupts before I can say any more. "That's for a client of mine," she says. "I told her to hire your dad to do her website."

"You thought your dad and my mom were getting married?" Samantha laughs. "That's so three months ago!"

Dad and Paige look at us, confused, and Samantha changes the subject fast. "I don't wanna talk about this sappy stuff. Come on, let's go. I wanna ride the Claws of Doom!"

"Claws! Of! Doom!" Larry cheers.

Samantha's mom nods. She says she'll take Sam and Larry there, and suggests we meet up in a few minutes. That's fine by me. As fun as the Claws of Doom sounds, I have a million questions going through my mind for Dad and Terri. I attempt to "prioritize" (something I learned in

Focus! class—it means putting the most important thing first) and ask a good one. "Are you two in love again?"

Dad and Terri look at each other. "You wanna answer that one?" he asks her, and she laughs.

"We didn't *stop* being in love," Terri tells me. "Love is a feeling you have inside; you can't really control it. You can't make it happen, and sometimes you can't get rid of it even if you want to."

That sounds terrible, I think.

"But there's a difference between being in love and being in a relationship," Terri continues. "That's the part your dad and I need to work on."

Ugh! I never thought of this. It seems hard enough to find the person you want to be in love with; then there's another step? This is all sounding like a big, annoying waste of time. I think I'll stick with my friends and my drawings.

"When did this happen?" I ask. The second of my million questions.

Dad and Terri exchange glances, looking a little unsure. "Well, it was nice to see Terri at your art show," he begins.

"So I asked to come over and pick up my pot—you know, the one we cooked beef bourguignonne in. . . ."

"We couldn't find the pot, but at least we started talking," Dad says, smiling.

I have to smile too! The potion we made in the pot *did* bring Dad and Terri together—just not in the way I thought it would!

I'm about to move on to the third of my million questions when I notice something different about Dad. I don't know if it happened just now or earlier in the day, but it's there, right in front of me. Or to be more specific, it's *not* there.

"Dad, your . . . uh . . . your necklace," I say. "It's . . ."

Dad puts his hand to his neck. "Oh no, I had no idea! It must have fallen off."

"It's okay," I say. "You can tell me you got rid of it."

"But I didn't!" he assures me. "I really liked that necklace! I'm sorry. I have no idea what happened to it. Maybe you can make me another one."

My mind is a mash-up of a million more questions, and there's no prioritizing them. Did our Siren Calls work? Did *any* of the charms work? Did Ryder Landry get my message in a bottle? I guess none of it matters right now, because (1) Ryder Landry was here, (2) Madison's my friend to the end of the Earth, and (3) Dad and Terri have their arms wrapped around each other's waists. They look good together. Maybe they have to work on their relationship (boring!), but at least they're still in love.

I won't be making Dad another necklace.

Dad and Terri walk with me to the Claws of Doom. A mechanical black claw rotates around in the sky like the hand of a giant pterodactyl—except hanging from this pterodactyl are a bunch of pods spinning around with people strapped inside. We pass Paige texting on her phone, and she points us toward the front of the line, where I see Madison, Samantha, Larry, Lisa Lee, Kylie Mae, Ronnie, Lonnie, and some other kids from sixth grade. A few of them wave and shout to me.

"Can I go?" I ask Dad.

"Sure," he says. "Go be with your friends."

Friends. The word has never sounded so good.

Terri gives us a ride home, and I get right in the backseat without having to be asked. Even with my seat belt on, I can lean forward enough to stick my face between them. They'll have plenty of time to spend with each other; right now I want to ask Terri if she's coming over tonight and if she has any special plans for the summer, and I tell them they can have a date tomorrow night because I'm staying over at Madison's but maybe the next night we can all play a game or something, and Dad tells me that I'll see plenty of Terri this summer and to calm down. "It's been a long night," he says.

It's also been the best night ever and I don't want it to end.

Then it ends.

I must have fallen asleep, because the next thing I know, Dad is unbuckling my seat belt and tapping me on the shoulder, saying we're home. I sleepily ask if Terri is coming in, and she says yes. She and Dad are going to stay up and talk for a while.

I can totally walk into the house by myself, but I act really sleepy and hang between Terri and Dad as we walk up to our door. I go to my room and change into my pj's, and a few minutes later, there's a light knock at my door.

I lift my head off my pillow and manage to say, "Come in."

In the little bit of light coming in through my window, I see two shapes in the doorway. Not Dad alone, but Dad and Terri. "I know when you turn twelve you're going to be too old for this," Dad says, "but we wanted to say good night."

I sit up and reach my arms out. Dad comes over and gives me a hug with an extra squeeze at the end. Then I gesture for Terri to come over too. I give her a hug and tell her good night, hoping there will be lots more nights like this in the future. I'll know that she and Dad are together down the hallway, laughing and talking and playing Pig Mania and maybe even kissing if they want to, as long as I don't have to see it too much.

BANG BANG BANG BANG BANG!

A loud sound makes me sit straight up in bed. I look down at the floor and see Toby glancing up at me lazily, nowhere near as startled as I am. I look at my clock. It's 3:33 in the morning!

"What the . . . ?" Dad shouts. I hear his bedroom door open and the sound of him shuffling down the hall.

I hop out of bed and run to my door. I open it and peek out. If there's somebody dangerous out there, maybe I can create a diversion so nothing bad happens to Dad.

"Who is it?" Dad says in a loud, tough voice that sounds nothing like him.

"You know who it is, Bradley! Who else would it be?"

I recognize that voice. It's a man's voice—a voice I haven't heard in many weeks. He's only communicated by postcards. And now he's here. When everything's over!

My dad opens the front door and I run down the hall-way. Toby follows, happily barking. "Uncle Arnie?" I shout.

Yep. It's Uncle Arnie all right.

His frizzy gray hair, sticking out in all directions, only has a few streaks of black in it. He's a very sloppy dresser, in a T-shirt that was once white but is now more of a brownish gray, with a slightly ripped flannel shirt over it and baggy jeans that his belt is not holding up well.

"Sorry for the late arrival, baby brother," he says. "Can you pay the taxi?"

Both Dad and I look past Uncle Arnie to a taxi at our curb. The light is on inside and the driver is staring at us.

"Please don't tell me you took a taxi here from New Orleans," Dad says, almost whining as he walks to his desk and picks up his wallet.

"No, no, no! What kind of crazy fool do you think I

am?" Uncle Arnie winks at me as Dad heads down to the taxi. "I *am* a crazy fool," he whispers, "but not that kind."

"I know," I say. "I've been getting your postcards. They've been very inspiring."

"Oh, that is sweet, little Cleo!" he says. "How old are you now, that you know a word like *inspiring?*"

I tell him I'm eleven, almost twelve. "So big!" He sounds surprised, which is strange because he sent me the voodoo doll as an eleventh birthday gift—though it *was* seven months late. Oh well, that's Uncle Arnie!

"Where's the most comfortable place in this house to perch my butt? Is that it?" he asks. Without waiting for me to answer, he strolls into the living room and plops himself down on our couch. I sit on the edge, too shocked and excited to settle in.

"Uncle Arnie, I waited for your instructions and I wanted to be patient but I couldn't stand it anymore, so I tried to call you but there were two strange women at your house. Well, one was strange and the other was more normal but they thought I was a ghost child and—"

"Oh, that was probably my cleaning lady and her daughter. I let them stay at my place while I came on this fantastic adventure!"

Tonight I saw Ryder Landry in person, realized I have more than two friends, learned that Dad and Terri are back together, and found out Uncle Arnie's love potion might have worked . . . but the most shocking thing might be

finding out that he has a cleaning lady. I have more important things to ask about right now, though. "What adventure? Where have you been?"

"You got my postcards, so you know! Louisiana, Texas,
New Mexico, Arizona, and now Californ-I-A! Two thousand
miles of excitement and adventure, close calls and good times!"

A journey of two thousand miles, like on the postcard!
Uncle Arnie was writing about his own journey! "I left New
Orleans behind, at least for a while, and saw this great land
of ours. I rode the rails, and I caught rides with all sorts of
people. I worked a few days here and there and used the
money to take the bus to LA. But I didn't know how to get
here—to your house—in the middle of the night, so I had
to splurge and spend the big bucks on that taxi outside."

Actually, it's my dad who's spending the big bucks, but
I don't bother bringing that up.

"How long are you staying, Uncle Arnie? What are you
going to do here? You have to meet my friends. Madison
and Samantha are my best ones, I guess, but Larry is really
funny. And maybe someday I'll like Lisa Lee and Kylie Mae;
I don't know. And I have to tell you about . . ." I stop and
look around quickly to make sure Dad's not back. "The love
potion," I whisper.

"We'll have plenty of time to do it all, don't you worry!"
says Uncle Arnie with a booming laugh. "But right now I
think I need to change into my jammy jams and get some
shut-eye."

He stands up and looks toward the front door, right as Dad walks in. He's got a big blue duffel bag over his shoulder. "That was one expensive cab ride, Arnie," Dad tells him, dropping the bag to the ground. "And maybe you could've brought in your own luggage."

Uncle Arnie runs over to the bag. "Be careful with that, Bradley! There's some precious cargo in there!"

Precious cargo? I run over to it too. "What is it?" I ask. "Can I see, can I see?" I can't believe how wide awake I am now, considering how tired I was earlier!

"It's three-thirty in the morning, Cleo, and you've got school tomorrow," Dad says.

"Not really! It's the last day!"

"Let me show Cleo one little thing, Bradley, and then we can all hit the hay." And Dad really has no choice, since Uncle Arnie is already kneeling down and unzipping his duffel bag. He starts pulling stuff out and tossing it on the floor, not thinking about Toby and how interesting he finds things like flip-flops and socks. Sure enough, Toby bites into a pair of smiley-face boxer shorts and runs away.

Dad shouts at Toby, but Uncle Arnie tells him not to worry. "Those weren't my only jammy jams, Bradley." He tosses a few more items on the floor—a squeezed-out tube of toothpaste; a raggedy stuffed animal that looks like Fuzzer, his cat at home—and then he finally finds what he's looking for.

It's a rectangular wooden box, a little smaller and squarer

than a shoe box. It's polished all shiny, but I can tell it's not new. There's gold trim around the edges and a metal lock on the front.

"A treasure chest?" I ask.

"It's a treasure chest, all right," Uncle Arnie says. "And there's some very intriguing information inside. But it's too much to get into tonight."

What? There's nothing else I want to do but hear more about this treasure chest! Tomorrow's the last day of school; we're not going to learn anything! It doesn't matter if I'm tired or not. I make all these arguments to Dad, but he's not listening. He tells Uncle Arnie to pick up the stuff he threw on the floor, and he tells me to go to bed.

I give Uncle Arnie a hug, then Dad. I want to stay up and talk to them until sunrise—to tell them all the things I've learned about friendship and the universe and last-ditch efforts, and then ask questions about the things I don't understand at all, like magic and love.

But I have to go to bed. There's one more day of school and a long summer ahead, and a treasure chest full of "intriguing information" sitting in the living room, and a party at Madison's with my friends, which may eventually include Lisa Lee and Kylie Mae—who knows? Stranger things have happened.

No one knows that better than I do.

Acknowledgments

This book was an exciting challenge, and so much fun to write. As always, there are many people to thank for their help.

✦—My agent, Jen Rofé, who advised me to rewrite a wackadoodle first draft into something so much better

✦—My editor, Caroline Abbey, who made this second book experience unbelievably smooth and wonderful. Can they all be like this, please?

✦—My family, my friends, and my coworkers at *The Real Housewives of Beverly Hills,* for their enthusiasm and encouragement

✦—And Tim, my Canadian from Cambodia, for understanding when I spent so many late nights at coffeehouses instead of coming home

Brendan Holmes

No stranger to storytelling, TONI GALLAGHER earned a journalism degree from Northwestern University and has a successful career in reality TV. She began as a story editor on the early seasons of MTV's *The Real World* and was a producer on the beloved Disney Channel show *Bug Juice,* about real kids at summer camp. Currently she is executive producer of *The Real Housewives of Beverly Hills* on Bravo. Toni lives in Los Angeles and loves finding the magic in it. Visit her at tonigallagherink.com.